The Innocents
and Other Stories

GERTRUD VON LE FORT

The Innocents
and Other Stories

TRANSLATED BY
MICHAEL J. MILLER

IGNATIUS PRESS   SAN FRANCISCO

From the original German titles:

"Die Unschuldigen" © 1960 and
"Die Verfemte" © 1960 by
Deutsches Literaturarchiv, Marbach

"Die letzte Begegnung" © 1959 and
"Der Turm der Beständigkeit" © 1957 by
Insel Verlag, Berlin

The translator thanks Elizabeth Schick for
preparing a fine draft translation of one of
the novellas in this volume.

Cover design by John Herreid

Photoreproduction of a drawing by Philip Henry Delamotte, c. 1850
From the digital archive of the Rijksmuseum, The Netherlands

Contents

The Innocents

*In memory of the children
who died in World War II*

We have escaped as a bird from the snare of the
fowlers; the snare is broken, and we have escaped!

—*Psalm 124:7*

I STILL REMEMBER WELL how Uncle Eberhard would take me on his arm when I was a little boy—at that time he still wore his black uniform. "Lad," he used to say, "would you like to fly?" By that he meant that he wanted to throw me high up into the air and catch me again.

"No", I replied. "Flying is scary." I was not thinking then about Uncle Eberhard's intention, though, but about the nights in the city when the sirens had wailed so horribly to say: The foreign airplanes are coming!

"Hello, what do you mean, 'Flying is scary'?" Uncle Eberhard exclaimed. "Flying is a magnificent thing, my little lad!" He wanted to say more, but Mommy was already signaling to him that he should not talk with me about flying.

That was eight years ago, and the war has been over for a long time. I am not a little child now; I am a big boy—twelve years old soon. Yet even today, Mommy never talks with me about airplanes—I know she wishes

7

I would forget all about the sirens and the airplanes. But I cannot forget them, although my thoughts always go only up to the edge of the memory—when I try to think of the most terrible moments, then suddenly there is a big hole, as dark as the cellar where we were sitting then, and there is such a terrible droning noise that I can no longer think about anything. Then all I hear is Mommy's voice, loud and clear as a shout through all the other shouting: "Mary, take my child into your arms!" Then for a while everything is gone—all I know is that someone held and carried me.

When I began to think and see again, I thought at first that it really was the Virgin Mary holding me in her arms because Mommy's face was as black as the picture of Our Lady of Altötting that hung in her room. But soon I noticed that it was Mommy's face, covered with smoke and soot, completely frozen with fear and terror and yet as though neither those two things nor anything else existed in the world.

I asked, "Mommy, am I dead now?" Then her face flinched, and she began to weep so dreadfully that the tears drew bright furrows across her black cheeks and my face got all wet, since she was bending over me. That did me a lot of good because it was still almost as hot as it was before in the cellar and so dry that my face was burning.

We were sitting on a big pile of stones on a street I did not recognize. I did not know how we had got there. A big clinic stood across the street from where we had lived, and Mommy used to say that I was born in it. On the street where we were sitting now, there was no clinic, and our house was not there, either—all around was nothing but buildings that you could not recognize because they were lying on the ground. There was smoke, thick smoke everywhere you looked. The sun was just rising; its long rays fought their way through the smoke like Mommy's tears through the soot on her face—it looked as if the sun were weeping. Across the street from the pile of stones where Mommy sat with me, a row of dolls was lying on the pavement. Men with helmets climbed up out of the building that was lying on the ground and brought more and more dolls, which they laid down at the edge of the street. I looked at the men, while Mommy wept, and I began to count the dolls. But suddenly Mommy jumped up, turned my face toward her, held me tight, and dashed away with me. I have forgotten what happened next, and I do not want to think about it at all, for I know that Mommy is afraid that I might, and I do not want to alarm Mommy.

I know why Mommy is so worried. I recently heard Herr Unger, my tutor, tell her that I am an imperiled, physically backward child. And it is true, I am small and weak for my age, and sometimes I cannot think or speak as quickly as I would like—I can write better. They say that I get that from my father: he kept a diary from an early age; it is Mommy's greatest treasure, and she reads from it each day. Ever since I learned that, I have been keeping a diary, too; I want to give it to Mommy later as a gift—will she be as fond of it as she is of Daddy's diary? Maybe she will be happy that I am not just a backward child, but I think that Mommy has known that for a long time. She told Herr Unger then: "It is only the shock of that night that Heini has not gotten over; we must be patient a little while longer." Herr Unger has a lot of patience with me, but that is probably not especially hard for him because he always looks as though everything that happens does not matter to him at all.

Grandmama often says to Mommy, "It's a shame, Melanie, that you did not go right away with Heini to Hohenasslau when it started in the cities." By that she meant when the foreign airplanes started coming. Mommy then replies: "But we still believed that Our Lady of Käppele would protect us from the airplanes— in fact, the whole city confidently believed that—and yet she did not." Grandmama then said, "If she did not, then you probably did not pray enough."

That made Mommy angry, and suddenly she spoke very softly—Mommy always speaks very softly when she gets angry, and therefore most people do not notice it; but if you are fond of Mommy, then you almost fear her, or fear for her—I cannot quite tell the difference. But then Mommy had good reason to be angry because Grandmama did her an injustice: Mommy did pray very much when we were still in the city—often, when I woke up during the night, I could hear her rosary jingling, and she still had it with her in the cellar. She still had it wrapped around her wrist, too, when she sat with me on the stones, but after that I did not see it anymore—maybe she lost it when she dashed off with me. Sometimes I want to ask her about it, but I am not supposed to talk with her about that time.

I love Mommy so much that I can never say it, but she knows anyway. Sometimes people call me "poor child", when they think of my father, whom we lost in the war. Whenever that happens, I would like to speak up and say, "I am not a poor child because, after all, I have Mommy!"

I cannot describe Mommy. Sometimes I hear people say about her: "It is unbelievable that she's still so attractive, after all she has been through." But that is not right; Mommy is not "attractive"; she is beautiful, very beautiful, although when Uncle Eberhard says it to her, I feel like shouting at him: "You must not call Mommy beautiful; not you!" Uncle Eberhard knows it, too—once he held both my hands tight and said, "So, little lad, now as your punishment give me a kiss."

Mommy asked him: "What did he do wrong that he has to be punished?" Uncle Eberhard gave no answer but just said: "The boy knows what I mean." And that was right—I did know.

Even as a very small child I could not stand Uncle Eberhard, but now I wish that he were not there at all: I mean, that he had not existed in the first place. But he does exist, and every Sunday he comes to Hohenasslau—I think the castle where we live belongs to him. But maybe it belongs to Grandmama, too, I am not sure; earlier it belonged to my father. When Uncle Eberhard is there, he always says to me, "Isn't that right, Heini: you and I get along well together?" He would like to hear me say, "Yes, we two get along well together." And Mommy is supposed to think I am fond of him, but I would not say that for the world, and if I did say it, Mommy would not believe it.

Uncle Eberhard is tall and has broad shoulders and a long, narrow face and big white teeth, so that it looks as though a trap were set in his mouth. He cannot laugh properly with his lips; he laughs only with his teeth, just like a dog —our Barry laughs with his teeth, too.

When I said that recently, Grandmama blushed, lifted her eyeglasses, and turned to Mommy: "No. This is going too far. Melanie, I beg you: what will the future be if Heini opposes Eberhard in this way?" She wanted to say more, but Mommy signaled to her that she had better not continue—Mommy is always afraid that Grandmama might say something I should not hear. Grandmama, though, is not afraid of that at all. Yesterday, Mommy said to her: "Mother, you always forget that children today are much more alert than in your youth, or even more so than in mine. Seriously, nowadays they are really alarmingly alert—they have been startled far too early and far too cruelly."

Grandmama replied, "But Melanie, how quickly a child forgets!"

Grandmama does not believe what Mommy says about me, and Mommy does not like to quarrel with her while I am around. But in the evening when I am lying in bed and they think I am sleeping, they often quarrel with each other in the next room—I sleep in the little windowless space between Grandmama's room and Mommy's because, although the castle is very spacious, we live crowded close together due to the many refugees who have been housed in Hohenasslau. Grandmama cannot stand the refugees; she cannot forgive them for taking so much room away from her, and they are often loud and discontent. "They are ungrateful people", Grand-mama says. "If only they could be expelled!"

But Mommy replies, "Do you think that you and I would be grateful in their place? My God, what these people have been through!"

Mommy speaks often with the refugees and lets them tell her again and again about their plight. She learned their stories long ago, but she acts as though she were hearing them for the first time. She acts as if she herself had not been through anything, for the refugees always think that they are the only ones to have been seriously affected. Mommy lets them think that. "Then at least they enjoy their pain," she says to Grandmama, "and, after all, that is almost the only pleasure these poor people have."

I am actually very glad that I sleep so close to Grandmama and Mommy because the castle is very old, and all sorts of things have happened in it, so many people have already lived here. Earlier their pictures hung in the big hall where the refugees now eat. Mommy talked Grandmama into having the pictures taken down. "Often", she said, "the refugees have not been able to salvage so much as a photo of their parents, and it must make them sad to see that we can even look at all our ancestors." At first Grandmama would hear nothing about this plan, but finally she thought that maybe it was better for the pictures to be taken down—the refugee children might make mischief with them. Now all the pictures are standing in the attic, leaning against the wall. Only Captain von Asslau from the Thirty Years' War is left hanging because his place is not in the hall but in the stairwell over the first landing. This captain looks almost like Uncle Eberhard, although he does not laugh like him, but still, when you see him, you think of a vicious dog. Each time I walk up the steps, I am startled by his face. Then I have to think about the bell *Friederizia*, too, which the Captain donated to the convent in Niederasslau and never should be rung because otherwise some misfortune will take place: why, I do not know—there is something weird about it. Earlier there was also a ghostly child here that ran around the whole castle at night surrounded by flames. He has not been seen for a long time now; only the old refugee woman Krusza sees him now and again.

Krusza is supposedly not quite right in the head. Often at night she knocks on the floor for hours with her crutch, so that it can be heard throughout the castle and Grandmama cannot sleep. As she does so, she cries out ceaselessly: "Let me in! Let me back into my dear old house at last; that is the only place where I want to die!" But then she suddenly loses patience, throws the crutch away and screams terrible curses through the window into the night. Grandmama thinks they are meant for us because we still have a castle and a lot of fine old furniture, but Mommy says they are meant for those who drove Krusza out of her home and for others who did something terrible to her as she was fleeing.

Recently, when we met Krusza in the park, she said to Grandmama, "Has Madame noticed the strange child that always walks back and forth in front of the castle when the Colonel is expected?" The Colonel is Uncle Eberhard.

"What sort of child?" Grandmama asked.

Krusza shrugged her shoulders. "Ask him yourself, Madame, but do not come too close to him. Otherwise, you will catch fire like the poor people who were burned up on the asphalt in the beautiful city when we refugees were trying to stop there. Has Madame ever seen burning people?" But Grandmama was no longer listening; she turned right around and left the park so quickly that Mommy could scarcely follow her—fortunately they had not paid attention to me.

When we were in the castle again, Mommy said to Grandmama, "How strange that Krusza should claim to have seen that! After all, she cannot possibly know anything about the old legend."

"It is not strange at all", Grandmama replied. "Someone told her the legend, and now she would like to vex and frighten us with it—you can see that plainly from the fact that she tried to connect that unfortunate child with Eberhard."

I think that Grandmama was much fonder of Uncle Eberhard than of my father, who was also her son, after all. It made her proud that Uncle Eberhard is so tall and imposing—my father, they say, was not as tall and imposing, and that probably disappointed Grandmama. She herself is tall and imposing, too, much taller and more imposing than Mommy, but that is precisely what I cannot stand about Grandmama. Maybe it is because I myself am still so small and weak. But there is something else that Grandmama has against my father.

"You hold Karl's death against him, Mother," Mommy recently said to her—Karl was my father—"and yet it was a noble, heroic death."

"But not for a Christian", Grandmama replied. "A Christian must find another way out." Grandmama, I think, is very pious.

At that, Mommy said, her voice trembling, "You know very well, Mother, that otherwise Karl would have been shot according to martial law."

Later I asked her, "What does 'shot according to martial law' mean?" At that Mommy was quiet for a while, and then she said curtly: "It means: fallen in battle."

Mommy has beautiful blond hair, but since father's death there has been a white streak in the middle along the part. Grandmama urges her to have it colored, but Mommy does not want to. "You should do it for Eberhard's sake", Grandmama insisted.

"No, I leave it as it is for Karl's sake", Mommy replied. "Karl did not like anything that was inauthentic. This white streak is in memory of him." Again Mommy spoke very softly because she was angry about Grandmama's demand.

But Grandmama was also angry at Mommy: "Sometimes it seems to me", she said, "as though you have grown fond of Karl only since he died."

"I always admired Karl", Mommy answered.

"But as long as he was alive, you loved someone else", Grandmama continued.

At that Mommy said, and it sounded almost like a

threat, "Mother, there is something that looks like love and yet is not love."

I really believe that Grandmama is very pious: she rides every morning to Niederasslau for the early Mass, although the steward actually cannot spare the coachman and the horse on a workday—we do not have many horses because we are no longer rich. But Grandmama insists on her Mass, and she cannot travel the long way to Niederasslau on foot.

"This trip to church brings blessings to us all and to your management of the estate, Herr Köchele", she says. But the steward says behind her back, "What good are blessings to me when I need horses!"

On Sundays, Herr Unger and I accompany Grandmama to Niederasslau. I kneel between them in the manorial alcove near the altar, where many cherubs flutter around the columns like butterflies. I often have trouble praying because I prefer to look at the little angels. Grandmama, though, prays all through the Mass without looking up from her book; I always see how her sunken mouth moves zealously as she whispers. I do not know what Herr Unger does; I cannot imagine that he prays because in church he looks just as indifferent as ever.

Uncle Eberhard says about him: "He is one of those young people whose parsley crop was completely destroyed by hail. It is like that everywhere in our country: no more guts, no verve. Yes, indeed, today's youth has wilted!"

"Herr Unger did not wilt", Mommy contradicted him. "After the war, he bravely made something of himself although he nearly starved. I know that he even donated blood in the hospitals in order to earn money for his studies." Mommy always defends Herr Unger, just as she defends the refugees, and he knows it, too. Sometimes when she comes into the room unexpectedly, his small, pale face suddenly becomes red and warm, and he looks almost happy. I think he has a crush on Mommy. With Herr Unger, I do not mind that.

Mommy never goes with Grandmama to church in Niederasslau. Since she lost her rosary, she does not go to Mass anymore, either—she does not even go to the castle chapel when one is said there. But Mommy cannot stand the castle chapel at all because it is dedicated to the Holy Innocents. On the chapel wall to the right of the altar is a painting of the massacre of the children in Bethlehem. On the other side is the small head of a little Asslau who went off on the Children's Crusade. Both pictures are already so faded that they seem to be covered with spider webs. Only when the sun shines through the high, narrow window of the chapel can you see them clearly. The refugees say that the little Crusader resembles me, but Mommy will not hear of it because that little Asslau supposedly reached the Holy Land but never returned.

Now I know why I wish that Uncle Eberhard were not there at all, I mean, that he did not even exist!

Today there was another scene with the refugees: one of the women said that the big picture in the chapel does not show the massacre of the children of Bethlehem at all

—those little Jewish children had been killed somewhere else, and anyone who did not know where had only to ask the Colonel.

Grandmama was so upset about it that she was literally speechless.

"It would truly be a stroke of good fortune", she said, "if you could marry soon, Melanie; Eberhard will soon deal with these people."

"His way of dealing with them would frighten me", Mommy replied. O my God, I am frightened, too! What did Grandmama mean when she said that Mommy should marry soon and that Uncle Eberhard would soon deal with the refugees?

Something is going on that they are not telling me about —everyone seems to know about it except me! Even Herr Unger is changed: his small, indifferent face suddenly looks more alert—no, more disturbed than I would have ever thought it could look. That must be connected with Mommy somehow, because except for her he does not care about anything.

Even the refugees have noticed something. Yesterday, the old gardener chased the children out of the park because while playing they were throwing dry leaves on the paths that he had just raked. "Get out of here", he said. "Today the Colonel is coming to Hohenasslau, and the park has to be in order."

One of the old refugees, who was sitting peacefully on the bench, called to him: "What do we care about the Colonel? Little Heini is his father's heir; Hohenasslau belongs to him."

At that, I went over to the men and said, "No, Hohenasslau belongs to my Mommy, because if it belongs to me, I want to give it to her."

Now the refugees looked at each other strangely. Finally, one of them said, "If you want to give Hohenasslau to your mother, my little lad, just be very careful that Herr Eberhard does not settle down in it, too—for he would like very much to marry castles."

I cannot believe it. I cannot believe it, although Grandmama and Mommy talk about it every evening when they think I have gone to sleep. But I would not go to sleep for the world; I want to know what is going on!

"You should make your decision for Heini's sake", Grandmama said at last. "Heini is a problem child, and besides—a boy needs a fatherly hand." As if I did not do everything that Mommy wants! Mommy, of course, knows this. "Heini is not a problem", she said.

"But Karl thought of you, too, Melanie, when he expressed his wishes in the event of his death", Grandmama insisted. "Do you think he did not know your feelings for Eberhard while he was still alive?"

At that Mommy exclaimed: "Don't you understand, Mother? That that is precisely why I cannot!" And then, in utter desperation: "You just don't know, Mother, what you are asking. You just don't know!"

Two young apprentices disappeared from Niederasslau. People mutter that they went off with a foreign recruiting officer. I did not know what that meant, but the refugees explained it to me. We are not supposed to talk about it, but everyone does anyway. Grandmama was quite upset;

she talked about adventure-seeking and disgraceful abduction. Uncle Eberhard tried to reassure her, saying, "These young people have their reasons for going abroad. I have been thinking about it for a long time—there is nothing left here for the likes of us."

"For God's sake, Eberhard, you cannot be serious!" Grandmama exclaimed in horror. All of a sudden she looked piteously old and helpless. But Uncle Eberhard answered quite calmly: "Why should I not be serious, Mother?" As he spoke, though, he looked not at Grandmama but at Mommy, as if he meant to say: "It depends solely on you."

I will have to hear it from Mommy herself if I am to believe it! But how can I begin to ask her? When I was still little, I used to say to her, "I love you so much, Mommy. Can't I marry you when I grow up?" And she would only answer, "Oh, my silly child, my great big silly child!" I have known for a long time that I cannot marry Mommy, but now when I tried to ask her, I could think of nothing to say but the silly old question. So I said, "Mommy, do you still remember how I always wanted to marry you when I grew up?" She understood immediately what I meant and said, "Oh, my silly child, my great big silly child: we two belong to each other inseparably, whether or not I get married now."

"And with whom will you get married?" I asked. My voice trembled as I did, I was so afraid of her answer, but she gave none, and therefore I knew who it was.

I said: "Mommy, I cannot stand him, and deep down you do not like him, either—why are you doing this anyway?"

Then she looked at me very seriously and gently and said, "Because your father wanted it, Heini. I respect your father so much that I will do this for love of him even after his death. And now you, too, must do something for love of him and be nice to Uncle Eberhard. Will you do that?" When Mommy asks me for something, I cannot say no, whatever she may want of me. So I said, "Yes." But it was not the truth—I lied to Mommy.

Uncle Eberhard now sends flowers to Mommy every day by wire. She puts them on her little rosewood desk—and then it looks as though the desk were blooming. Since yesterday, Uncle Eberhard's picture stands alongside; in it he laughs again just like our Barry. When I saw the picture, I could not help myself, I had to grab it and throw it down on the floor. And then I tore up the flowers, too, and trampled on them. I cannot say how good it made me feel.

Right after that, Mommy came in and saw what had happened. She knew right away that I had done it. "Heini," she said, "didn't you promise to be nice to Uncle Eberhard? Why are you not keeping your promise? What do you have against Uncle Eberhard?"

I said, "He laughs just like our Barry, but he is much meaner than Barry. I think he can drop bombs." I did not know what made me think of bombs, but I knew that if I started talking about bombs, Mommy would end the conversation. And she did immediately; in fact, she did not even contradict me, so frightened was she that I was thinking about the bombs. But after that she put on again the pretty, bright-colored dress she has been wearing recently whenever Uncle Eberhard comes. Until then she still dressed in mourning.

I know that deep down Mommy still mourns my father. But when she is with Uncle Eberhard now, it sometimes looks as though he had forbidden her to be sad. For Mommy is entirely changed; she laughs much more often and much louder than she does otherwise, and I think that this laughter even hurts her. I cannot get to the bottom of it, though, because they send me away when they are together. Or rather, Uncle Eberhard sends me away; he no longer has any use for me; he no longer needs Mommy to think I am fond of him—he thinks Mommy is fond of him. And it looks that way, too— she even had the white streak of hair dyed! Yes, it really looks as if Mommy is happy now, but this sort of happiness does not suit her at all.

Mommy read something in the newspaper that Grandmama does not want to believe. "The newspapers always lie, Melanie", she said. "I do not understand why you take them seriously. Germans do not do such things; only the others do such things."

At that Mommy asked: what about Captain von Asslau, who after all was a German, too. Grandmama replied, "Good heavens, Melanie, those were olden days; nowadays such things do not happen."

But Mommy contradicted her in a soft voice. "Everything happens nowadays, just as in the olden days. Yes, I fear that much more horrible things happen than before. Have you already forgotten what we ourselves experienced in our own country?"

"I would gladly forget it," Grandmama replied, "but you do not do me that kindness."

"Poor Mother", Mommy said then. "There is no forgetting, because everything that happens is irrevocable, and so it is written in the old *Asslau Chronicle*. I should fetch it sometime from the pastor."

Mommy fetched the old *Chronicle* from the pastor and read to Grandmama from it. Grandmama did not want to listen at all, but Mommy said, "You must hear it, Mother. It could have been written today." She read aloud in a strangely solemn way:

> And so these terrible flames shoot up toward heaven, all the days and nights that God will allow until the end of time. Let no one presume to believe that this fire has been extinguished merely because even the greediest flame is finally satisfied and the most brightly glowing coal finally becomes embedded in the ashes. For nothing that has happened can be undone, and all that has commenced ceases not but, rather, continues to work secretly or openly, and its effects stop only before God's throne of judgment on the Last Day.

When Mommy had read that far, she stopped for a moment, then stood up, went to the door and listened for me. I lay as still as a mouse, as though asleep. Then she turned around and gently closed the door behind her.

The next morning the *Chronicle* was still on her little rosewood desk, and the bookmark from the evening before was still in it. So I opened to the page and copied it. But I had got only as far as I have written here when

Herr Unger appeared to take me on a walk. When we returned, the *Chronicle* was no longer there.

Mommy spoke about Captain von Asslau when she was about to fetch the *Chronicle*; I wanted to know at last the story of him and the bell *Friederizia*! Recently I asked Herr Unger about it. We were together in Niederasslau, for it is already Advent, and I wanted to buy something to give to Mommy at Christmas. Grandmama had given Herr Unger some money for it.

In Niederasslau, there is a gift shop with wax goods from Munich: many honey-colored candles, little red plaques, and colorful Nativity figures. We went there, and Herr Unger suggested that I should give Mommy a red wax medallion with the *Münchener Kindel* [the child on the coat of arms of Munich]. But I wanted to get a Christ Child. First they showed me one that was lying poor and naked in the crib, and then they brought the little figure they call "The Infant of Prague": He has a crown on His head and a scepter and an imperial orb in His hands, just like a little king.

"Why don't you want to take the Child in the manger?" Herr Unger asked.

I said, "I would like to have a powerful Christ Child, because Mommy has to be protected now."

Herr Unger saw the point—I mean, that Mommy must be protected—for since he, too, learned about her future marriage, his small, pale face has become even smaller and paler; you might think he had donated blood again in a hospital somewhere. He no longer contradicted me but brought out his purse and silently paid for the Infant of Prague.

Then, as we were going back home, the bells tolled to mark the start of Sunday. It was already rather dark, because the days in Advent are short, but they have a spotlight now in Niederasslau with which they illuminate the tower of the convent church so that it stands in the night like a tall, silent candle. Beneath the fat onion domes, we looked into the open belfry, where the two big bells swung mightily back and forth. But the third bell, *Friederizia*, hung motionless and silent beside them. I took the opportunity to ask Herr Unger about it, but he gave me no answer. He only said that there was something sad and terrible about its story and that it was better for us not to talk about it. Then I said nothing more because I think that Herr Unger was thinking about Mommy, who always worries that I might become frightened.

A very harsh winter set in early this year. In the park, the refugee children no longer fight their little battles with dead leaves; they use snowballs. There is much too much snow: it is very difficult for the hunters to feed the deer and the stags in the forest, and the steward is tearing his hair out over the firewood for the many refugees. Everybody says: If only the men who can do almost everything now would finally learn to regulate the weather, too! But Mommy says, "Unfortunately they have learned it already, because the weather is becoming ever crueler —nature is furious with us, and truly she has a right to be." With that, she pushed the newspaper toward Grandmama and said, "Just read it, Mother; unfortunately it did not lie."

On the last Sunday of Advent, Mommy put on the pretty, bright-colored dress again, when Uncle Eberhard was supposed to come, but then she wrapped herself in her big woolen shawl so that you could not see anything of the pretty dress.

"Take the shawl off", Grandmama pleaded with her. "You look so unattractive in it; it conceals your figure. Why did you wrap yourself up like that?"

Since Mommy gave no answer, I said: "Because Mommy is freezing in this world."

Then Grandmama once again lifted her eyeglasses and asked me: "Why do you say, 'in this world', Heini?"

I replied, "Because the dear Lord no longer makes the weather."

On Christmas Day, Uncle Eberhard was here and showered Mommy with presents, but I think she was not really happy about it. Uncle Eberhard's gifts crowded her entire Christmas table so thickly and arrogantly that my Christ Child was completely covered by them. I had to bring it out from underneath myself and put it in Mommy's hand. She did not recognize it immediately, because she said, "Oh, a little child with scepter and crown, a tiny little child with the imperial orb—how terribly moving!"

I said, "But Mommy, it is the Christ Child!" Now suddenly her eyes filled with tears. "Poor little Christ Child," she said, "have you ever been able to prevent anything cruel?" But then it probably occurred to her that I had wanted to please her, and she quickly kissed me on the forehead—my face became wet, as it did back then when we were sitting on the pile of stones and I was counting the dolls that the men had laid at the edge of the street. All at once I knew that they had been little dead children and that Mommy had thought of them when she saw the Christ Child. I do not know what Uncle Eberhard was thinking—he was probably annoyed because Mommy had tears in her eyes. Throughout the holidays he remained in a bad mood; everyone was glad when he departed.

Several days later, the Church celebrated the Feast of the Holy Innocents, to whom the castle chapel is dedicated. A Mass is celebrated there every year on that day, so that Grandmama for once does not have to go to Niederasslau. We all went with her to the chapel, Herr Unger and I and the castle domestics and many of the refugees. Again, Mommy did not go, although she had agreed to at first, but afterward, as Mass was about to begin, she had suddenly disappeared. The priest gave a sermon about the psalm verse from the liturgy of the day: "We have escaped as a bird from the snare of the fowlers; the snare is broken, and we have escaped!" The priest said that the verse expresses the voice of the Holy Innocents.

Suddenly one of the refugee women began to whimper audibly. "But the children did not escape at all; they froze! They lay motionless and stiff on the ice when we fled across the lagoon. They threw them into the water like dead fish!" She moaned so loudly that the priest had to interrupt his sermon until they had led the woman out.

Later, when we left the chapel, Mommy was standing on the stairs holding in her arms the woman who had whimpered before. She had nestled her head on Mommy's bosom and wept very gently and quietly. Later Grandmama told Mommy that she would like to explain to the woman the psalm verse that she had misunderstood. But Mommy just shook her head.

Now I know about the terrible thing in the newspaper that Grandmama did not want to believe. During the war, they killed a whole village in France! First they shot the men, then they set on fire the church into which the women had fled with their children—all of them were burned up inside as though in an oven. The most terrible thing is that Uncle Eberhard's soldiers were the ones who did it! Since Mommy learned this, she has been quite distraught. The soldiers are now on trial in France; every day there is a report about it in the newspaper. When Mommy has read it, she always becomes quite motionless, just like back then after the night of bombing when we were sitting on the piles of stones. Recently Grandmama hid the newspaper from her, and then Mommy went to Niederasslau and bought one at the kiosk. After she had read it, she said to Grandmama, "Eberhard must travel there and take the blame for this. He must stand by his soldiers; they were only carrying out orders—terrible orders! But he gave the order."

Grandmama replied, "Eberhard did not give the order himself; he was not even with the troops then."

"But he had supreme command of that squad," Mommy said, "and they did order such things—I know they did—after all, think of Karl's fate."

Grandmama replied, "That is precisely what I am thinking of. Such a journey would be certain death for Eberhard. How can you ask it of him?"

"Karl did not fear certain death", Mommy insisted. "He feared God, and you claim to be a pious woman."

"But you are unwilling to be one," Grandmama replied, "and that is at bottom the reason for all your trouble and unrest. God permitted this terrible event; if you could believe in Him, you would soon find peace."

"No, on the contrary, then I most certainly would not find peace," Mommy said stubbornly, "because if God existed, He would have to be as indignant as I. But there cannot be a God, because the whole world is full of the suffering of the innocent!"

"That is precisely how the world was redeemed", Grandmama said calmly. "The guilty merely get their just punishment, but the sight of innocent people suffering softens hearts—Christ suffered, too, although He was innocent. Until you accept that, you cannot be a Christian woman."

"And I do not want to be one", Mommy protested, again looking quite desperate. Grandmama, though, sat so upright and proud as though nothing and no one in the world could shake her.

I thought, "What Grandmama just said really sounded beautiful and mysterious. Why, then, will Mommy not accept it?" But then I recalled what Herr Unger recently said to her: "But what could be the reason why people today no longer believe the piety of pious people?"

When the newspaper started reporting every day on the trial in France, Uncle Eberhard stopped going to the park at midday when the refugees walk back and forth in the bright winter sunshine. He must have heard what they were shouting after him. They shouted, "Now we finally know why they bombed the beautiful city while we were trying to rest there as we fled. The way you treat others is how you will be treated!"

Grandmama no longer walks in the park, either. She prefers to stroll on the steep path behind the castle, although it is very fatiguing for her. Not a ray of sunshine reaches it, and the ground is so slippery that it seems to be all ice and no earth. Mommy is always afraid that Grandmama could slip and fall there.

Mommy and I walk now as usual in the park, and no one shouts anything after us. Just yesterday, when I was alone there, looking for the refugee children because we were going to make a snowman together, suddenly Krusza appeared behind the snow-covered yew bush and cried, "Be careful, little Heini, for the strange child is back again who would like to take the Colonel away! Do not come too close to him; right away he will start to burn like the poor people in the beautiful city when they dropped the phosphor bombs on us. Phosphor bombs are bombs that cause an inextinguishable fire; it is a hellish fire."

Uncle Eberhard now talks a lot with me again. Yesterday, he said, "Heini, Christmas is past, but once again

you must confide a wish to me—what would you like
from me?"

I replied, "That you travel to the place where Mommy
wants you to go."

Now his long, narrow face swelled up with anger, and
he pushed me away so roughly that I almost fell.

"Where did the urchin learn that?" he shouted, looking at Mommy. She answered him not a word but took
me by the hand and led me out.

We went up to the attic, for anywhere else in the castle
or the park you can run into the refugee children. The
attic is quite deserted; the only things living there are the
jackdaws that build their nests there in the summer. It
was cold in the attic, but Mommy had her big shawl on
again; she wrapped one half of it around my shoulders
and drew me close to her. Then she sat down with me on
a box and looked at me reproachfully with her big, gentle
eyes. "Heini," she said, "you have been eavesdropping!"

I replied, "Why did you not tell me yourself? After
all, I am not a silly child anymore; I wanted to know why
my Mommy is worried and upset."

She replied, "And I did not want my silly child to be
worried and upset. Oh, Heini, dear child, forget what
you heard! It is too terrible; you must not imagine it."

I said, "Mommy, I can very well imagine it of Uncle
Eberhard, but why were the soldiers all like him? Why
did they obey him?"

"Because otherwise they would have been shot according to martial law", she said.

Now suddenly something occurred to me: "Was this
order the reason why they shot Daddy?" I asked quickly.

She replied, "Not this one, Heini, but one like it."

"And Daddy did not want to carry it out, right, Mommy? He preferred to let them shoot him?"

She was startled, she hesitated, and I saw that she was looking for some escape. But then she told me honestly and decisively, "No, Heini, your father shot himself, but his death was nevertheless a noble one. Your father preferred to die rather than to kill the innocent."

"Why couldn't Uncle Eberhard's soldiers shoot themselves, too?" I asked.

"Because they were not your father, Heini. Your father is one of a kind, because it is very difficult to shoot yourself or to be shot. Maybe you cannot yet imagine that; how could you, my poor child."

I said, "I can too imagine it. After all, that is why Uncle Eberhard does not want to travel; he would rather be cowardly and disloyal."

Now we were silent for a long while. The jackdaws flew in and out through the open skylight, we sat there so still. Mommy had wrapped the shawl even tighter around me. My head lay nestled against her heart. It beat very loudly, so afraid was she of what I would say next. I was afraid of it, too, but I had to say it, nevertheless. "Mommy," I asked, "when Daddy shot himself, did he already know who Uncle Eberhard was?"

She replied, "I don't think so, Heini. At that time Uncle Eberhard was still with another division, and you must not think that all our soldiers received such terrible orders. The officers in the other regiments were chivalrous in the foreign land, yes, certainly they were. You must not think ill of German soldiers. Never forget that your father, too, was a German soldier." She repeated that several times very fast. Meanwhile the jackdaws still fluttered around us. Suddenly she interrupted herself and cried, "Oh, if only we could fly away like them!"

I knew she wanted to escape my question. "Do you think, Mommy," I said trembling, "that even now Daddy would still want you to marry Uncle Eberhard?"

She replied, "I do not know, Heini. I really do not know." Then once again: "Oh, if only we could fly away like the jackdaws!"

"But I know", I said.

I experienced something wonderful: I became acquainted with my father, whom I never consciously saw. It is as though he spoke with me and entrusted Mommy to me, for he can certainly no longer entrust her to Uncle Eberhard! And now I must make sure to rescue Mommy. But it will be difficult, because after all we are not jackdaws that can fly away! And in the attic I not only became acquainted with my father, I became acquainted with Mommy, too: I understood how terrible it is that she can no longer escape Uncle Eberhard.

For several days I have dreamed each night about an invisible fire that threatens Mommy. I cannot help thinking of the poor women and children in the French church— they could not escape Uncle Eberhard, either; it is just as terrible for my poor Mommy!

My only hope of rescuing her is for Uncle Eberhard to travel to France after all and for this trip, as Grandmama said, to be his certain death! I wish the French would kill him! But he will not travel, for he does not care at all that Mommy dreads him. He will not let her loose, I think; it excites him to hold her against her will. It is like a battle between the two, but Mommy is much weaker than Uncle Eberhard; he will force her to marry him, and she will not admit to herself that he is forcing her—she will make herself believe that she is doing Daddy's will: my poor Mommy is that helpless!

The foreign recruiting officer is said to have been in Niederasslau again; nobody has seen him, but everyone claims to know that he has spoken with Herr Unger, too. Mommy shakes her head, and Uncle Eberhard laughs when anyone speaks about it, but in my opinion Herr Unger really looks as if he would rather just go away, for he too has come to understand Mommy's situation. At first, as the trial began, it seemed to give him some hope. I believe that he thought that Mommy would not marry Uncle Eberhard, now that such a terrible thing about him has been made public. He looked forward to the trial that was to bring this about. Poor Herr Unger, poor Herr Unger, yes, maybe it would be good for him if the foreign recruiting officer took him along! From now on I must be very nice to Herr Unger.

Yesterday I walked into the room just as Uncle Eberhard kissed Mommy—she did not resist; I think she kissed him back. I closed my eyes so that she would think that I had not seen anything, but she probably did not even see that I was there. Then I went away quietly.

That evening as she came to my bed as usual and bent over me, I could not help turning my head toward the wall, I was so afraid of Uncle Eberhard's kiss that was

still on her lips. It was only a very small movement that
I made toward the wall, but Mommy understood it in-
stantly. She became very pale and was about to step back.
Then I quickly put my arms around her neck and kissed
Uncle Eberhard's kiss away from her lips.

Grandmama now no longer says, "Germans do not do
such things", but she no longer reads the newspaper, either. The last time she did, it reported how one of the German soldiers on trial in France exclaimed, "I am ashamed
of my officers, because they are not here!" Then Grandmama closed the newspaper and put her eyeglasses aside.
I saw her eyes open wide and her demeanor almost col-
lapse, like that of a very old woman—I had never seen
that before! I thought: Now she, too, knows that Uncle
Eberhard must travel to France, and now she will come
to Mommy's aid. But she did not; she kept talking as
usual about Mommy's wedding. I think that she, too, is
in Uncle Eberhard's hands, just as inescapably as Mommy,
only in a different way. My pious, stern Grandmama is
a mother; she cannot be separated from her son, just as
Mommy could not be separated from me.

Mommy, too, can no longer bear the newspaper reports
about the trial now, but the refugees can bear them. That
is strange, because they themselves have already experienced so many terrible things. When I go at midday into
the hall where they are eating and bring them the apples
and nuts that Mommy gives me for them, they are always
reading aloud the reports about the trial. Today they were
passing around a page from a newspaper; on it was a picture of a French woman. She stood in the middle of the

ruined village that Uncle Eberhard's soldiers had burned down: not a single human being was with the woman, only dead houses, as terrible to look at as our street had been back then after the night of bombing—I now know that it was our street after all! The refugees said that this woman was the only human being who was able to escape from the burning church; she jumped out the window, but her children and grandchildren were all burned up.

"One child is still burning", Krusza exclaimed, but the others paid her no attention. "This French woman", they said, "reportedly has never laughed again since then, and she will certainly never laugh again even if she lives to be a hundred."

I wanted to say, "But Uncle Eberhard still laughs with his teeth just like our Barry!" But just in time I saw Barry's kind, loyal dog face: he was wagging his tail and going back and forth simply among the tables, begging. The refugee children rumpled the Saint Bernard's thick coat, and he patiently put up with it. Then I said nothing more but asked Barry for forgiveness.

It is as though Mommy lives two lives now. By day she is Uncle Eberhard's fiancée, and you notice nothing unusual about her, except that her hands often twitch in a peculiar way, as though they were trying to grasp something that they could hold on to, if only a blade of straw. But by night a completely different Mommy appears, who walks back and forth and back and forth for hours in her room. She also whispers as she did earlier when she could still pray, but she is not praying, she is only speaking to herself. Sometimes in the dark, when she comes into my little bedroom and remains standing by my bed, I even catch her words—they are always the same: "A child like this one," she whispers, "a child like mine—no, many, many children like mine—and he caused their death . . ."

Then I wish more than anything that I could put my arms around Mommy's neck again and kiss away Uncle Eberhard's kiss forever, but I think that Mommy is only saying all that in her sleep, and I am afraid to wake her.

Krusza is not afraid to wake Mommy. Last night she suddenly came down the stairs, pounding with her crutch, and along the corridor up to Mommy's door. She struck it with the crutch and called, "Young Lady, lock up good, because now the foreign child has already come into the castle."

I must become the blade of straw that Mommy can hold on to!

Mommy has to be separated from Uncle Eberhard; it is necessary that I bring this about, and I know how, too. I said to Mommy, "Couldn't we become two jackdaws after all and fly away? Couldn't we travel to France instead of Uncle Eberhard? After all, you could visit the poor woman who was pictured recently in the newspaper. She was so sad and lonely standing in the burned village—our city was burned down, too, and you too were made unhappy by Uncle Eberhard—you belong together. Couldn't you tell her that?"

Now Mommy was very startled—for a while she could not speak at all. Finally she said, "No, darling, I could not tell her that at all, because compared with that woman I am infinitely wealthy—I have you."

Now I finally know the story about Captain von Asslau and the bell *Friederizia*! The wire service had sent flowers again from Uncle Eberhard to Mommy—very beautiful, almost white roses, with only the faintest hint of dawn in the depths of the calix. But Mommy was startled by the roses: "They come from France," she said, "these are Malmaison roses." She told Herr Unger and me to take them to the nuns in Niederasslau.

As usual, it was very cold, and we had to pack the roses carefully. As Herr Unger was tying string around the carton, Mommy unexpectedly came in, but now he no longer blushes happily when he suddenly sees her; he becomes angry. "I hear that you have caught a cold", Mommy said in a friendly tone. "Can you tolerate the trip to Niederasslau in winter, dear Herr Unger?"

"I can tolerate other very different trips," he replied without looking up from the carton that he was tying, "and you can be sure that I will tolerate them well. Very well, in fact—nothing more can bother someone who has been cured of his ultimate madness!"

"But Herr Unger, that sounds almost like a categorical renunciation", Mommy teased.

At that he made a stiff, somewhat comical bow. "I thank you, Madame", he said, and then he quickly went out to get his coat. We set out on the way in silence.

After we had dropped off the roses at the gate to the convent, Herr Unger asked me whether I would like to wait a while for him in the church; he had another errand at the post office, and it is tiresomely slow there in this season because of the many skiers staying in Niederasslau. I could tell that he wanted to get rid of me.

When I entered the vestibule of the church, the old sacristan Moser had just arrived to toll, for it was already getting toward evening. It occurred to me that he must know about the bell *Friederizia*. So I said, "Herr Moser, why is this bell never rung?"

He replied, "Otherwise the masters of Asslau go mad."

"And why do they go mad, Herr Moser?" I inquired further.

"Well, now," he said, "that goes back to Captain von Asslau, whose soldiers burned down a church during the Thirty Years' War, together with all the people who had taken refuge in it. Well, it was a Spanish regiment that the Captain led, and the Spaniards were accustomed to burning heretics—that evidently pleased Herr von Asslau: they say that when he heard the wailing of the poor people in the church, he laughed. When the tower started to burn, the bell fell down, and the Captain brought it with him and gave it to the convent church back home in Niederasslau as a present. But someone probably put a curse on that bell: when they rang it the first time in Niederasslau and the Captain came into the church to hear Mass, the sound drove him out of his mind—he suddenly began to laugh, as he had done in front of the burning church, and he could never stop until he had laughed himself to death. And so, they say, it will happen to any Asslau if he hears the bell *Friederizia*."

Now at last I know what has to happen! And I am glad and confident. Everyone notices that something about me has changed. Today Grandmama said, "I think that now Heini has really got over the shock of that horrible night; he looks perfectly splendid." Herr Unger absent-

mindedly agreed; he had scarcely listened to what Grand-
mama was saying. I would so much like to confide my
plan to him, but I think that I must not tell anyone what
I intend to do; I must act all alone. Yesterday, though,
I almost gave it away to Uncle Eberhard. I asked him,
"Are you not sometimes afraid of the bell *Friederizia*?"

He looked at me with eyes wide open, then put his
hands on his hips and began to laugh out loud. "The bell
Friederizia, poor boy! And I am supposed to be afraid of
that! What sort of nonsense are you imagining?" Meanwhile he looked at me so strangely that I was deathly
afraid because I thought that he had an inkling of my
plan. But right afterward he went out whistling merrily.

Today there was another Mass in our castle chapel. It
takes place every year on this day; no one really knows
why, but so it has been for ages.

The older domestics think that it is offered in honor
of the little Asslau who went on the Crusade but did
not come back—they consider him a saintly child. The
younger ones, though, will not hear of it, they laugh about
it. Grandmama will not hear of it, either; she says, "That
little Asslau is only a legend in the first place." But I do
like to think that he lived and was a saintly child.

We went to the chapel, again without Mommy. I had
intended to ask the little Asslau to intercede on behalf of
my plan, but it was a very dark winter day, and the chapel
was so gloomy that at first I could not even recognize his
head on the old picture. Nevertheless, I looked at the
wall where I knew he was depicted and began to pray
for his help. Little by little, the wall became brighter, as

though light hands were removing a spider web from it, and the little Asslau emerged from the wall, and behind him many other children, too, who accompanied him. He smiled at me, and I think he really looked just like me; indeed, I had the impression that I myself was depicted in the painting, too. I thought: He will stand by me, because he has accepted me in his troop.

We had an awful scare, because since yesterday evening Herr Unger has vanished without a trace—they say that now the foreign recruiting officer has taken him away, too. Grandmama is terribly annoyed. Mommy is very quiet; I think she now knows what I have known for a long time. It is good for my plan that Herr Unger is no longer here, for tomorrow Mommy wants to go with Uncle Eberhard to Niederasslau and request the announcement of the banns. They will be right next to the convent church then so that I can carry out my plan. Without Herr Unger's supervision, I can get there unnoticed. Nevertheless, I say, "Poor Herr Unger, if only he had been patient for one more day!"

I will wait until Uncle Eberhard and Mommy have left Hohenasslau. They will take the country road; the snowplow has cleared it, and it is easy to travel. When they are out of sight, I will try to get ahead of them by taking the foot path through the woods. There is still a lot of snow there, but the hunters who feed the game have tread a narrow path. If I stick to their trail, I can be in Niederasslau before Uncle Eberhard and Mommy.

At this time of day, it will be very quiet on the square in front of the convent church. In the open vestibule beneath the bell tower, it will be easy not to notice someone coming across the square. Herr Moser will not be tolling at this hour. Just recently I looked very carefully at the three bell ropes hanging there. Two are worn and old; these are the ones that Herr Moser and his boy have to pull; the third is probably much older but not worn at all. I will take this third rope in hand, and then I will wait until Mommy and Uncle Eberhard come across the square. I am a little afraid that the rope could break because it is so old and it looks like a dry, crumbled hemp plant. And the old bell is very heavy, and it has been still for so long —will it awaken and let me move it? Little Asslau, help me! *Friederizia*, righteous old bell, let me move you!

From here on Frau Melanie of Asslau records the feverish words of her child:

I am lying in bed, and Mommy is sitting beside me— how did I get here? I can no longer remember! Mommy, will you not help me? I was just in Niederasslau waiting in the bell tower for you and Uncle Eberhard.

You came across the convent square walking very slowly. Uncle Eberhard was speaking very eagerly to you—and you listened, smiling; he demands that of you, and you looked up at him obediently and smiled. Oh, how I hated him on account of your smile! Suddenly I was no longer afraid at all that the rope might break; nor did I fear that the bell would remain mute. Granted, at first she did not want to ring—she had probably slept too long—maybe the clapper had rusted, maybe I did not have enough strength. I had to hang on the rope with all my weight— my feet no longer touched the ground: instead of me moving the bell, she moved me. Finally, though, she started to ring—slowly and heavily, as though she were opening a serious, stern mouth and making short, muffled sighs, stopping again and again for a moment as though she had to draw a deep breath. I was so out of breath that I heard it as though from a great distance— my heart was beating like a hammer against my chest— there was a rushing noise in my ears, so that the bell tone was almost smothered by it. "Louder, louder, *Friederizia*, louder, louder, because I cannot do this much more!"

Suddenly Uncle Eberhard was standing in front of me—he bared his big white teeth at me. "Hello, little friend," he said, "I thought you were the one ringing this damned bell! Bravo, that's just right! But now let me at it!" He took the rope from my hand. "Now, watch carefully how I ring *Friederizia*." He laughed again, baring the big white teeth in his mouth.

Mommy, he laughed horribly, but he was not mad, he was not! Had *Friederizia* lost the power to punish him as she had punished Captain von Asslau back then? Does something like that not happen anymore today? I suddenly dreaded Uncle Eberhard so much—I wanted to hold my ears when he rang—I wanted to run away— he noticed it and commanded me: "Wait right here, if you please, my lad, and listen! And then we will see what happens—because you are an Asslau, too!"

He was not holding me, and yet I could not move. I wanted to call to you, Mommy, but then you appeared already in the archway and stretched out your hands to me breathlessly. O, Mommy, you were as white as snow, you feared so much for me! I wanted to run to you, but it was as though my feet had been taken away from me. And then the bell was already thundering as though it were trying to burst the vestibule and the tower. Meanwhile I heard high, desperate laughter, but it was not Uncle Eberhard's laughter—I do not know who laughed like that—Mommy, can't you tell me who laughed like that? Did someone else go mad instead of Uncle Eberhard? But there was nobody there except you and me—or—or—was that not laughter at all—was that a scream, the way the people screamed back then in the cellar? O Mommy, now I remember everything again—the terrible thing I was supposed to forget, because then another bomb came down on us with rubble and debris.

"Heini, it was not a bomb, it was the bell *Friederizia* that fell from the tower; she had completed her work; she will ring no more."

"Did she hit Uncle Eberhard?"

"No, darling. Nothing and no one can hit Uncle Eberhard."

"But why, then, did Grandmama weep so bitterly at my bedside? I never knew that she could still weep like that! And why did she then tell you that she can now understand why you no longer want to pray?!"

"Darling, Uncle Eberhard is gone, and that broke her heart . . ."

"Did Uncle Eberhard travel to be with his soldiers after all?"

"He left on the same journey that Herr Unger made, my child—he is not coming back."

"Well, does Uncle Eberhard not want to marry you anymore?"

"No, my poor child rescued me from that."

"Oh, then I am glad, Mommy. But why are you kneeling down all of a sudden? Can you pray again now? And why are they praying downstairs in the chapel? Is there another Mass today for the Holy Innocents?"

"It is the domestics and the refugees, darling. I think they are praying for you."

"Oh, that is kind of them, Mommy. I can really use it! Just think, soon I must depart—here come the children of Oradour already to take me—see, Mommy, these many, many children! Were there so many children in Oradour? And not one of them is burning now—they are all waving to me and smiling so cheerfully at me! Please, Mommy, do not cry like that—I myself am sad that I must leave you—we never wanted to be separated! Ah, Mommy, is there no one who can stay with you when I am gone?"

"Darling, do not worry about me—there is someone who will stay with me! The poor woman from Oradour, whom you saw in the picture; she will stay with me when you are gone!"

"She will? Did she come to Hohenasslau?"

"She does not have to come to Hohenasslau, and I do not have to go to Oradour—we are already very close to each other. And when you are gone, darling, we will be united."

"So that way you will not really be alone, Mommy?"

"No, Heini, I will never be alone again."

"So, now I want to go to the children—but suddenly I can no longer stand up—someone has to carry me. Ah, Mommy, if you can pray again, then please say once again: Mary, take my child in your arms . . ."

"Mary, take my child . . ."

The Ostracized Woman

> For the LORD . . . [will show] mercy
> to thousands of those who love me
> and keep my commandments.
>
> —*Exodus 20:6*

I NEVER SAW HER, though I often stayed in Golzow on visits in my youth, and I never spoke with anyone who could say that he had seen her, although everyone knew that there were some in the village who claimed to have seen her. But the people to whom such incidents happen have a profound dread of speaking about it—only after many years did they open their mouths; yet that belongs, not at the beginning of this story, but rather at its end. At the time, it seemed only legend could claim that, on certain days, she still stands before the door of the old manor as she once did when the young Swede fell at her feet. And the broad, bottomless marsh lay outside, precisely as it had then, beyond the mossy park walls; the so-called "Swedish Footpath" was still the sole way over the primal grounds of that beautiful, treacherous wilderness—one that was not without risk for the uninformed. The white tufts of the tussock cottongrass still beckoned at the edge of the black, insidious pools of water; the spectral mist still smoldered and hovered right up to the old manor at night and transformed the clear lines of its sober, stately structure into the ghostly ambiguity of its inaudible mysteries. And in the long row of family portraits decorating the spacious dining room of this house still hung the empty frame and, underneath, the small baroque nameplate with the ornate inscription: "Anna Elisabeth, Bride of Golzow, born 1654, widowed 1675. . . ." The year of death was missing—back then, they had already cut the portrait out of the frame and erased the remembrance of the one depicted.

From time to time, when they were among themselves, the family quarreled over whether they should not simply remove the empty frame, as its rather peculiar presence clearly disturbed the serene contentment of the house. It also frequently prompted guests coming from elsewhere to ask puzzled questions, which the master of the house— my uncle—usually evaded dismissively and indignantly. And if one knew the family, this was thoroughly understandable. The Junkers of the Markish district are— no, today one must say: they *were*—a conservative clan, and the centuries could hardly have changed their persuasions. My uncle, who was otherwise so chivalrous, would likely have behaved toward Anna Elisabeth very much as his forefathers had done two hundred years before. Here invincible forces of persistence were in play, a persistence that certainly also contributed to the fact that the empty frame, despite all objections, still remained hanging where it had hung for two hundred years.

As for me, I was rather a bother to the Golzowians because I felt a juvenile interest in the empty frame and the ostracized Anna Elisabeth that became quite intense upon meeting opposition. No one, however, was inclined to gratify it, for, as I said, the Golzowians did not like to speak about this chapter of their family history. Even my indulgent aunt turned a deaf ear when I asked her, albeit for a very different reason from that of my uncle: "You cannot understand this story until you yourself are married", she was wont to reply to my cajoling —everyone knows that elders were indescribably prudish toward young women back then; they would have preferred to see them still believing in storks.

Barbara, my cousin of my same age, apparently knew no more about Anna Elisabeth than I did. "We just disown her", she said when cornered by my questions, whereby her childlike, naïve face took on a trapped, almost fearful expression. I was exasperated with her, for I had a different trickle of blood in my veins from that of the Golzowians. For me, this meant a nearly irresistible impulse from early on to go against the flow, to defend the oppugned, and to eulogize those who are suspect.

"Aren't you ashamed to disown someone you know absolutely nothing about?" I asked provocatively.

Now something stirred in the apathy of her small, well-bred character. "But I *do* know about Anna Elisabeth", she blurted. "I have heard the stories that Trina and the other maids tell! They still believe today in the village what Anna Elisabeth believed."

"And what did she believe, then?" I queried.

"That a woman can go wrong when a dead man is in the house." And then, turning red: "Anna Elisabeth was expecting a child when the Swede came."

Well, that was of no help to my investigation, either. The Swede—a child? What did they have to do with each other? And what did that mean: go wrong?

"I think it means: harm the child", Barbara stammered —she obviously had a terribly guilty conscience about our discussion. And then there was nothing more to be pumped out of her. I had to take matters into my own hands; maybe Hans-Jeskow would help me with it.

Hans-Jeskow, Barbara's adolescent brother, who adored me at the time in a boyish, rough manner, was the only Golzowian who occasionally sided with me and supported my questions about the disowned ancestor. Yes, once he was even willing to spend an entire afternoon rummaging with me through a remote attic, in which, according to an unfortunately baseless rumor, the portrait that had been cut out of the frame was said to be located under all sorts of old clutter. Sometimes, when the three of us rambled through the fields, he even deigned to accompany me to the so-called Melliner Cemetery, where the Golzowians allegedly interred their unpopular ancestor so as not to have to tolerate her presence in the family crypt.

The Melliner Cemetery provided the resting place for a Huguenot colony that the Great Elector had once settled there. The village of Mellin had disappeared, the colonists had long since migrated to the surrounding villages, leaving behind only their dead. Surrounded by a thick box hedge as high as a wall, this lonely resting place exerted a certain charm on me in and of itself, but, above all, I was concerned about the grave of Anna Elisabeth. With Hans-Jeskow, I untiringly brushed apart the long, fine forest grass, always in the hope of coming across a sunken stone bearing the sought-after name. But these graves had probably never even had stones, and the simple wooden crosses that may have been erected for the exiles had long since crumbled away. Only pale scabiosa and blue bellflowers adorned the forgotten graves, and here and there grew a crown imperial lily half-choked by forest grass or a rosebush run wild.

Meanwhile, Barbara stretched herself languorously on the other side of the box hedge in the shady grass. She never accompanied us when we visited the Melliner Cemetery—I sometimes had the impression that something in her resisted the memory of Anna Elisabeth, and today I know what it was, too.

"Why do you keep coming here, anyway?" she asked sullenly. "You ought to know by now that you will not find Anna Elisabeth's grave."

"All the same," I retorted, "this is a good place to think about her, since it is the cemetery of the displaced. And after all, she is an outcast, too."

Now suddenly she looked at me with huge, appalled eyes that swallowed up all the naïveté of her childlike face. "But I do not like to think about displaced people", she gasped. "Losing your home must be terrible! That must be the most terrible thing in the world!"—Oddly enough, her words stuck in my memory—or perhaps it was quite natural, as I have never seen people who were so unquestionably and primordially attached to their plot of land as the Golzowians, although they hardly ever spoke of it. You could tell by the fact that they were unimaginable anywhere else except in Golzow.

We sat then for a while longer in the shadow of the high box hedge. It was comfortably cool there, and the sweet scent of a nearby lupin field permeated the air. "We have to soak it up, quickly and thoroughly," I said eagerly, "because the inspector intends to have the lupins plowed up tomorrow—it is so sad for the pretty flowers!" Hans-Jeskow laughed at me: only someone who came from the city could say something like that! Meanwhile Barbara had composed herself.

"If Anna Elisabeth was disowned by us, then it served her right", she said defiantly. "My father says she was a traitor, and that must be true. Otherwise she would not haunt us!"

"Why don't we stay up one night and keep watch for the ghost?" I suggested.

"That will not work", Hans-Jeskow said. "We do not see the phantom—only the villagers see it."

"Do they really see it?" I asked, as his answer sounded rather uncertain to me.

"Yes, they see it", he replied, now very definitely. "Anna Elisabeth stands at the threshold of the house and waits."

"For whom is she waiting?" I wanted to know. Now he hesitated.

"Yes, for whom does she wait?" he repeated. Obviously the question had occurred to him for the first time.

"Maybe for justice to be done in her case", I insinuated.

He looked at me with astonishment. "You mean, she is waiting for us?" he said. Then suddenly he jumped up: "Oh, nonsense!" Then he put on the Golzowian landowner expression, and I could get nowhere with him for the moment. But he did not sustain it for very long, and so he was the one who brought to my attention a little later the so-called "Chronicle", who was supposed to come to Golzow soon.

The "Chronicle", or, as my uncle used to say, "The Book of the Chronicle", was the nickname of a poor, aristocratic spinster who rented a small apartment in the neighboring district town but was hardly ever to be found there. The Chronicle was related to all of the rural nobility in the area either by blood or by marriage, and the manors jumped at the chance to invite her over, for her nickname was accurate, inasmuch as she truly was a living chronicle of the whole area and was therefore a most entertaining guest. She could wind up the confusing yarn of the knottiest kinships so neatly that one instinctively thought of Ariadne's thread; she understood the derivation of that fine, ancient fabric that we call traditions; she could provide information about the estate of each clan in Brandenburg, about its castles that were still standing and about those that stood no longer; and of course she was well acquainted with the austere, proud sacrifices made by these old families. She could recite the long list of their sons who had fallen in battle as far back as Frederician, yes, even Electoral times. But she also knew about the secrets of the heart and the silent tragedies of these people, who were outwardly so cool and unimpeachable.

A veritable firework of anecdotes rose to the surface when she came to speak of certain eccentrics in these families. But neither did she shy away from reports of the minor and major scandals that had occurred here, as in every other place on earth where people dwell. Indeed, people even claimed that she did not mind—no, occasionally she even took pleasure in—shocking society somewhat. The Chronicle even had her own standard by which to measure worldly fortunes, errors, and catastrophes, as she knew much about people that one normally did not know and perhaps could not know at all. That is why my uncle, who enjoyed arguing with her, claimed that she fibbed a bit—and with that, of course, he came far closer to the actual secret of the matter than he himself knew. Contrary to popular belief, what really made the Chronicle into the "Book of the Chronicle" was not really connected primarily to her social and familial interests but was the result of an extremely charming talent for storytelling. It was also rumored that she secretly tried her hand at writing, which is why my uncle tended to characterize her as an aesthete—a title that, when pronounced by him, was joined with a slightly disapproving tone: Aesthetes, strictly speaking, did not belong to the group that he referred to as "our own".

I cannot say anything about what the Chronicle wrote —in Golzow, there was nothing to be learned on that subject. My uncle read the Christian newspaper in the morning and the Bible in the evening; besides that, he sometimes studied the Gothaer news and the sports section as well as a hunting and forestry magazine. My dear aunt, though, hardly managed to read anything more than the Bible quotes of the Baptist Brethren Assembly; what time she had left after caring for her own family was swallowed up by the large family of manor workers. Incidentally, my uncle's disapproval of the Chronicle as an aesthete was entirely theoretical in nature: in practice, he acknowledged with everyone else that she was actually a "charming person".

She appeared in Golzow for the military maneuver days: diminutive, amiable, and unconventional; whether she was old or young I dare not venture. To my seventeen years, she naturally seemed to be ancient, but today I would scarcely subscribe to that judgment. But above all, she seemed to me very different from all the people I knew. I was immediately captivated by her, yes, and in my amazement I idolized her because she managed to be so different and yet so well liked—in fact, society even celebrated her; a paradox that still frustrated me on a daily basis for the time being.

In Golzow at the time, two military staffs and a squadron of hussars were being quartered: the manor house and farm buildings were full to the roof; moreover, heavy artillery was bivouacking on the spacious estate. All hands were in motion, all feet flying up and down the stairs, but no one complained of fatigue. All the employees were exhilarated; for the girls in particular, nothing was too much, and their cheerful singing could be heard from dawn to dusk. Barbara and I, too, had to rub the sleep from our eyes at the crack of dawn in order to help prepare breakfast for all the hungry mouths. But once the many hundreds of slices of bread had finally been buttered and garnished, the last cups of coffee had been poured, and the provisioned men had happily marched out, then we were allowed to hitch up the carriage horses as a reward —oh, no, what am I saying? Not as a reward: in Golzow everyone did his duty without any claim to special prizes.

The famous slogan, *Travailler pour le Roi de Prusse* (Work
for the King of Prussia) was still in effect there—a phrase
that my uncle was proudly fond of quoting. Anyway, to
put it plainly: the carriage horses were hitched up, and
the open hunting carriage was driven at a graceful trot
down the avenue lined with ash trees and out into the
maneuver area, which extended for miles, like the moor
landscape, but in the opposite direction over the harvested
fields. Even from afar, you could hear the bright military
trumpet signals that called to and answered each other
through the clear, calm, soundless autumn air. Then the
troops came into sight.

We stayed close to the small hill where the command-
ing officers had set up their formation. My uncle, armed
with binoculars, eagerly followed the military movements
and, in doing so, fondly recalled his own years of service,
while Barbara and I peered out from under the billowing brims of our big straw hats at the lean junior officers. They greeted us from time to time as they rode past
our carriage and explained the colorful spectacle from
atop their prancing horses—for at that time the regiments
still wore their colorful uniforms: hussars and dragoons
gleamed in the pale fields of stubble like great leftover
islands of poppies and cornflowers. But the cuirassiers
looked the most splendid of all, especially those from the
guard, with their armor glittering in the sunlight and the
flying eagles over their silver helmets. On orders from the
highest-ranking officers, they even set out on splendid,
noisy cavalry charges, although everyone knew very well
that such attacks would no longer occur in future wars.

But who was thinking of war at that time? Certainly

not we young girls! For us, the maneuver days were pure celebration. Barbara in particular was beside herself with excitement; all her sweet apathy had disappeared. In the evenings, the officers were usually still ready to dance, while the regimental band played "The Blue Danube" outside. Barbara and I flew from one arm to another; each of us was an unrivaled belle of the ball, although the diminutive Chronicle now and then accepted an invitation for a ceremoniously billowing waltz—a secret agreement obviously existed between her quick feet and her wingèd words. Of course, the opportunity I had longed for to listen to her presented itself only on the final evening the soldiers spent billeted in Golzow. A kind of boredom with dancing had set in among the officers. After the late dinner, some had gone hunting with my uncle and Barbara, while others had ridden off to visit in the neighborhood or had gone for a swim in the forest lake.

For the first time, I was alone with the Chronicle, as my aunt had naturally been called to the village again. While we prepared together the old crystal glasses for the farewell punch planned for afterward on the terrace—these precious glasses were never entrusted to the servants—I deliberated on whether I should now ask for the story of Anna Elisabeth. It was so quiet in the house and on the terrace that you felt you could hear the first autumn leaves softly falling from the tall linden trees in the park. And from time to time the old crystal glasses clinked very gently and melodically against each other when the Chronicle's hand and mine touched while we worked. Without a doubt, now was the right time to present my wish to her. But I had the strange feeling she already knew of it, for each time the crystal glasses clinked against each other, she looked at me as though we shared a secret. Had Hans-Jeskow set something up for me so that I might be in her good graces? The good lad!—he was so terribly jealous of the officers! Or did the Chronicle really sometimes know something that actually could not be known? Did she know something about me, too? The only certainty was that, even though my curiosity had thoughtlessly importuned all the others, with the Chronicle, I could only wait humbly. Yes, the outcome of waiting seemed almost to be a test of the secret that resonated between us. And in fact: when we were finished with the glasses, she took my hand in her small, energetic right hand and pulled me down next to her on one of the comfortable wicker chairs and began to talk. It was already growing dark on the terrace, but a candle burned in the dining hall to which the double doors stood open —its glow fell squarely on the empty frame. And yet, it was as though the missing portrait now emerged from it. I relate it here as it has remained in my memory over the many decades.

A few days after the Battle at Fehrbellin, as the Swedish army frequently had to leave behind scattered, individual horsemen during their hasty retreat, who were either slain by the embittered peasants or were chased by the Brandenburg Regiments into the swamps, a very young, dead-tired Swedish cornet pounded on the gate of the Golzow manor. When it was opened, he recoiled, horror-stricken, for he had expected to find a detachment of his own comrades-in-arms, which had been based there until a few days before. Instead, he faced a sinister-looking man in the peasant garb of the country, whom he must have recognized as a doubtlessly hostile Brandenburger. The man then immediately slammed the manor gate shut behind the Swede and bolted it with the heavy beam.

"Just come in, you miserable wretch!" he cried. "You murderous arsonist and cattle thief! We know your kind well! We are going to give you a good Brandenburg welcome, so that you never again feel the urge to cross into our Elector's land." Then he let out a whistle, whereupon two stocky farmhands appeared in the doorframe of a visibly empty barn. "Jochen and Heinrich, grab your flails", the man at the gate called to them. "Here's work for you!" The young Swede—whose pistol had naturally shot its last bullet long ago—tried to grasp for his sword, but the other man's powerful fist prevented the exhausted soldier and held his hand fast.

A terrible realization dawned on the young man's face —he turned white as a sheet. And now the two farmhands were already moving closer, armed with their flails. At the same time, the door of the manor opened and a woman appeared on the threshold. Her face, still young, yet austere and careworn, was framed by the streamers of a white widow's cap. At the sight of the Swedish uniform and the unambiguous posture of the servants, she hastily retreated into the house, apparently willing to leave the public enemy to his fate. But before she could close the door behind her, the soldier, with the last of his strength, wrested himself free from the Brandenburger's grip. He rushed after her into the interior of the house and tumbled down at her feet. In his mortal fear, he pressed ever closer to her body, raising his hands imploringly to her. In doing so, he became aware that her womb was blessed, and he stammered in imperfect and strangely inflected yet still forceful German: "Mother, you are a mother! Save me!"

Perhaps it was the appeal with the sweet title of "Mother" that Anna Elisabeth heard addressed to her at that moment for the first time in her life—in any case, she remained standing and did not repel the supplicant.

But the three men in the yard had also rushed after the woman into the house. The one who had opened the gate for the Swede—probably the caretaker of the manor—cried: "My gracious lady, this is a public enemy and dealing with him is men's work—retire to your bedchamber! You are with child—take care that you do not go wrong!"

A transformation seemed to have occurred in the demeanor of the careworn woman. "Draw back," she replied, "and leave the stranger in peace. He is a conquered enemy and can do us no more harm."

"What good is a conquered enemy?" the other blustered. "A conquered enemy can come back again; what matters is a *slain* enemy!"

"What matters is the mistress of Golzow", the woman said imperiously.

"Yes, and doubtless the gracious lady's husband who fell in the war with the Swedes no longer matters?" the man asked insolently, but clearly he did not dare to carry off the man kneeling at the feet of the mistress. "Well, that is fine, too. We can wait, can't we, Jochen and Heinrich? The bloke there will not escape us." He exchanged a malicious look with the two servants, whereupon all three made off.

No sooner had the woman been left alone with the young Swede than the exhausted soldier completely collapsed. He fell prostrate on the floor, stretched out, and closed his eyes.

Now we do not know what went through Anna Elisabeth's mind in this hour—we know so little about her! In the short report on her that was later drawn up for the electors, her maids attest that she had hated the Swedes bitterly and had cried day and night since her husband's death and had not even wanted to take comfort in the child in her womb. Rather, it was as though she could not even tell that she was pregnant. And so it really does seem as though the awareness of her maternal hope flared up in her for the first time through the appeal of this young, desperate man. Perhaps her young, careworn face smiled in that hour for the first time in a long while. Perhaps— we do not know.

As it began to grow dark in the chamber—the almost full moon was still hidden behind the high barn roofs— there was a knock on the door. The woman opened it, and the old maidservant Stina slipped in on bare feet, clogs in hand. She cast a malevolent glance at the sleeping Swede, then whispered to the mistress: "Young lady, that man must leave! The electors will be here tomorrow morning and will kill him, and it serves the damned Swede right! But it must not happen *here*—a slain man in the house of the pregnant woman, that means disaster for the child."

"Yes, he must leave during the night", the woman replied quietly.

"But he will not get out of the house alive", the old woman retorted grimly. "The servants intend to stand watch the whole night and ambush him. You will have screams if they kill him in front of your door. I will let him out through the little cellar door and show him the way into the marsh."

"Do you think he could still reach his own men through the marsh . . . ?" There was something unfathomable in the woman's question.

"Maybe, maybe", the maidservant cackled. "Yes, if the marsh lets him through! But the marsh lets no one through who does not know his way around—it does away with everyone who walks without a guide, at Dead Man's Pass, if not sooner. But there, you will not hear it when it happens—the marsh does it without screams."

The woman was initially very still. Her face lay deep in the shadows of the silent twilight. Finally, she said sourly but very calmly: "Yes, there I will not hear it when it happens."

Then she added: "Go to bed, Stina, I will let him out through the cellar door myself." And, when the maidservant hesitated, brusquely and imperiously: "You understood me, so go!"

Once again, we do not know what went on inside of Anna Elisabeth as she was alone once more with the young Swede. Did she wrestle with the thought that he belonged to those at whose hands her husband had received the fatal bullet? Who was to say that it had not been at the hand of this very Swede? Was she willing to save him a second time—had the appeal to her motherhood transformed her so maternally even toward him?

The moon had now risen above the barn roof; its mild light fell into the vestibule and onto the face of the man slumbering on the floor. He lay there, thin and blond and young—much too young for the war—much, much too young. Between the white-blond eyebrows stood a bold, painful crease: a sign of the mortal fear he had endured. He lay there as though grievously wounded, having no mastery over himself, in sleep helpless as a child—nearly as helpless as the child sleeping under the woman's heart. No, we do not know what she was thinking—we only know what she did.

She waited a long time. The yard dog was still pulling at his chain, the barn door was still creaking, the steps of the watching servants were still creeping around the house. Finally, the night hid the last willful sound in its silence: weary heads sank against the front door—when Anna Elisabeth listened carefully, she heard the breathing of the sleeping men, innocent and deep as those of the nearby fields.

She lit no lamp, but rather brought bread and milk out of the cellar by moonlight, the austere meal of the land that had been sucked dry. Then she awakened the Swede and told him to take refreshment. He obeyed mutely; he was still drunk, as it were, from sleep and exhaustion. Only when she ordered him to follow her did he hesitate briefly, but then he seemed to recall how she had protected him earlier, and he followed her without protest.

Through the little cellar door they descended into the former moat in which a small baroque flower garden was now nestled. Its fragrance in the warm June night was like one big summer bouquet. The moon poured itself out in streams of light between the trimmed box hedges. Here and there a sharp stone glistened brightly as though moistened by water trickling over it—it was still dangerous here. But soon came the stairway in the garden wall; over its mossy steps one could climb up and down into the open countryside without a gate. And now the night fog of the nearby marsh began. They could still recognize shrouded alder trees and pastures. Once an enormous stag stood in the middle of the path, its dark antlers hovering in the mist like a ghostly crown. But soon there was a rustle in the alder shrubs, and it disappeared. A silent canal appeared; peat was piled up beside it; a black boat floated in the water as though ready to push off to the netherworld. Then the boat and the peat swam away; everything became impenetrably thick and gray as though the faces of the wanderers were covered with a cloth. And now Anna Elisabeth must surely leave the Swede to his fate, if she had adopted Stina's plan? Or had they not yet reached the right place? Again, we do not know what she was thinking—again, we only know what she did: Anna Elisabeth went on.

The path now became as narrow as a tightrope; the air was thick and humid, but still warmed from the heat of the previous summer day. Only occasionally did it suddenly become severely cold, as though an icy hand extended lightning-quick out of the ground toward the wanderers. In the distance, a toad croaked like the poor soul of someone who had sunk in the marsh.

They walked silently: in the lead, the woman trudged calmly, while he followed in her footsteps, still half asleep and as though dazed. It gurgled under their feet; water sprang up and leapt over their shoes like cold frogs. It smelled like reeds and bog. Occasionally, he had the obscure sense that the figure in front of him was merely a figment of his imagination or else that she could dissolve into one at any moment. Then again it seemed to him that she, too, was not quite sure of herself or of the way —he saw by the streamers of her widow's cap how she moved her head, uneasily peering ahead, but it was all as though in a dream, without substantiality or true awakening.

In the distance, a cry now sped across the marsh as though it wanted to color it blood red. Was a predator choking another animal, or did the cry come from a human throat? Had they chased another straggling soldier into the swamp? Anna Elisabeth listened: no doubt, those were Brandenburger gunshots, and those were the cries of the public enemies. And now finally it must have been clear what Anna Elisabeth was thinking, now she had to decide whether she truly wanted to rescue the Swede. For these gunshots—they rang out again and again in the distance—these gunshots were, so to speak, the voices of her own people, the exhortations of those to whom she belonged and to whom her beloved husband had belonged —yes, these gunshots were actually the exhortations of the Fatherland itself that struck her Brandenburger conscience, making stern demands, as though the hands of her deceased ancestors were knocking on her heart. Yes, now she had to decide; now she was finally shaken out of the sweet dream of her maternal joy; now she was, for the first time, fully aware of what the Fatherland was demanding of her.

But the Swede, too, had heard the distant shots. He had come to a halt: "Woman, where are you leading me?" he asked—that was the first thing that he had said on the journey. He sounded alert, almost frightened. Had the soldier suddenly leapt up in him, the soldier in enemy territory who could trust no one? Or had a somber spark of her distress flown over to him? Suddenly shivering, she turned around—she had the feeling he could strike her down from behind. For several seconds, she faced him as though paralyzed. She could not recognize his face in the fog, she could not even remember his face—it was as though they were both surrounded by evil spirits. And where a moment ago there had been a poor, dead-tired boy who was following her guilelessly, there was now an enemy, whom she should destroy and who could destroy her—or could he not, somehow, because she could not? Had the decision already been made?

They were now standing directly before the spot where the so-called "Dead Man's Path" began, the spot that Stina had meant when she said, "The marsh lets no one through who walks without a guide." If she were to say to the Swede now: "Go on confidently, from here on the path is no longer dangerous", he would surely believe her. He would then grope his way a short distance farther while she headed home, but then again a cry would speed across the marsh, more terrible than the one she had feared in her house. For Stina's words, "The marsh does it without screams", would have been true only if she had stayed home and left the Swede to Stina. The cry would not have mattered at all to Stina had she been the Swede's companion—she would have been gladdened and uplifted by it. For Stina carried no child under her heart, but *she* did —or was she really carrying only one? Were not two entrusted to her? The life of her child was dependent on the life of this Swede, and just as the latter had appealed to her as mother, so too did her child now appeal to the mother in her on the Swede's behalf, so to speak. Yes, God knows the decision had been made: she had already sacrificed the Fatherland when she had sent Stina away! But the Fatherland could never, never forgive her, and she would never, never be allowed to forgive herself.

The Swede now asked a second time: "Woman, where are you leading me? Are you even sure of the way?" It sounded even more urgent than the first time, and yet she felt that the evil spirits had already disappeared. She could remember his face again now, the way she had set eyes on it before in the vestibule of her house: so blond and young—much too young for the war, yes, truly pitifully young! And now, defenseless and heartbroken, she had to take the guilt of this pity upon herself. "Are you sure of the way?" he had asked; "Yes, I am sure", she said. "Give me your hand, because many have drowned at this point."

They now continued silently on the path. Finally, the ground began to solidify; they felt rustling heather under their feet. The fog became clearer, a sand dune protruded; it no longer smelled of reeds and bog but, rather, of junipers, resin, and thyme. Then a pine plantation rose out of the already-dawning light like a long stretch of low wall. Behind it, the glow of fire rose to the sky.

Anna Elisabeth stopped. "Over there", she said, "are the

campfires of your comrades. Head for them—nothing more can happen to you from here on." She turned back into the marsh; in the distance another shot was now fired.

"But you, woman," he called, suddenly understanding her situation, "something may happen to you! You guided an enemy; you will be punished! Have you no husband who can protect you?"

"My husband fell in battle", she replied gruffly.

"In the Swedish war?" he asked, keen-eared.

The streamers of her widow's cap trembled like wounded bird's wings. Without turning back toward him, she kept walking. He grabbed at her garment, which was damp from the fog: "And in spite of that you saved me, woman? In spite of that you were merciful to me?"

She protested: "Not I—my child saved you; a woman who carries a life that is on the way cannot allow death in her house." Fiercely, she snatched her garment from his hand. He ran after her and grasped it a second time: "May God then bless this child who saved me, and all his children and children's children. May they fare as I have fared, should they ever fall into the hands of an enemy. May God protect them down to the furthest generation!"

Then the mercy of her heart finally overpowered her: she was suddenly as joyful over the rescue of this young Swede as though the child in her womb had received a brother. Quietly and gently she said, "God bless you, too —you were the first to call me Mother."

The sounds of the new day arose as Anna Elisabeth returned through the marsh. The toads' croaking had fallen silent; the bitterns had awakened. The warble of the oriole rang out. A flock of wild ducks, crowded close together, flew overhead, flapping loudly. Small frogs and turtles leapt hastily over the narrow path. Anna Elisabeth had to take care not to trample the abundance of living things with each step she took—she felt a desire, which she had never known before, to spare even the most wretched creature. Even over the marsh the fog was now clearing. The ruddy sunrise made the solitude of the horizon bloom. Its delicate reflection lay on the black puddles of water; beautifully winged, metallically gleaming dragonflies darted over them; myriads of small insects whirred around the brownish flowering rushes. The reeds had become animated in the morning wind —they swished and sang as though with beautiful, wild harps. The simple landscape no longer emitted anything sinister or enigmatic; everything seemed decorated for the festiveness of the new day. Anna Elisabeth felt the desire to sing. She knew that she was carrying her rescued child home, but not only this one. Rather, it was as though this small child were growing under her heart and craving more and more of its space—as much space as if all people were supposed to find a place in it. Instinctively, she recalled the old legend from the Catholic era about the man Christopher, who carried the Christ Child over the water and, when he reached the opposite shore, realized that he had carried the whole world. Does perhaps everyone who is filled with mercy essentially carry the Christ Child? And now the war was over, all its injustice forgiven and all its suffering reconciled.

During that same day, a Brandenburg patrol arrived in

Golzow searching for a young Swedish officer who was alleged to have carried important information about the retreat of the enemy army. Whether the one they were looking for was the Swede whom Anna Elisabeth had guided could never be clarified; the only certain fact was that she had lent aid to the enemy and that he had saved his one flank. As the story goes, they wanted to court-martial her for treason, but the Prince-Elector, grateful for the victory he had just won and mindful of the fact that the young woman was expecting, magnanimously dropped the case.

Anna Elisabeth gave birth some weeks later to a healthy baby boy. Different opinions circulate about her subsequent fate. The family chronicle is completely silent about it. Some claim that, for years, she led a lonely, mournful life as a sort of prisoner of her brothers-in-law in a remote chamber of the Golzowian manor and later was buried in the Melliner Cemetery. Others claim that she died giving birth to her son or shortly thereafter, and, thus, no one could do anything more to her except take her portrait out of the frame and erase her memory from the annals of the family.

The Chronicle had finished. While she was still telling the story, the individual groups of our maneuver guests had returned from their outings and had seated themselves on the terrace. Chairs were moved, punch glasses poured, my uncle audibly cleared his throat—only the Chronicle did not let this disturb her in the least. Did the passion of storytelling carry her away so that she did not notice at all what was going on around her, or did she once again take some small, rakish pleasure in shocking her surroundings? In short, she continued to narrate unselfconsciously, and of course everyone was too well-mannered to interrupt her. When she had finished, there was an embarrassed silence—I knew that everyone was now thinking: "How can this small, unmarried person even mention such a topic?" No doubt, they felt embarrassed, but being polite, no one expressed it; rather, the criticism arose on a very different point.

"Very delightfully recounted, my gracious lady", one of the older officers spoke up. "But, by all that is right and fair, your heroine was still guilty of high treason: she protected the public enemy."

I was already prepared to pounce. "No, she conquered him!" I exclaimed zealously. "The Swede was no longer a public enemy when he bid her farewell and wished that her children might one day be saved just as he had been!"

"Now we Golzowians do not need that", my uncle burst out. "That, thank God, is provided for!"

"That is what we are here for, Herr von Golzow!" one of the young officers exclaimed.

"Yes, you fine lads in blue, that is what you are here for!"

The voice of my uncle, otherwise so dry, sounded unusually warm, almost moved.

"And that is what we will always be there for!" came the response.

"Long live Prussia!"

"Hooray, hooray!" cried Barbara. She looked excited and a bit comical, a little Brandenburger bacchante. All raised their glasses and clinked them. And now the regimental band in the park began to play a farewell serenade: the Hohenfriedberger March resounded—once again the proud regiments of the maneuver days seemed to march past us. Or was it not only these? Was it not instead all of Prussian history—in the form of sound and rhythm—that now rose up before us in this sparkling, glittering music? They had selected a medley of army marches—surely in deference to my uncle's preferences: The Hohenfriedberger March was followed by the Torgauer March and, then, by the march commemorating the triumphant entrance after the Siege of Paris. In conclusion, the Prussian national anthem was intoned, and all those present on the terrace sang along.

I can still hear it resounding confidently, as powerfully solemn as a vow, almost like a hymn over the darkened park out into the carefree, slumbering, unspeakably peaceful countryside:

Sei's trüber Tag, sei's heitrer Sonnenschein,
Ich bin ein Preuße, will ein Preuße sein

[Whether the day be cloudy or full of cheerful sunshine,
I am a Prussian, and desire only to be a Prussian]

When the last note had faded away, all rose to take their leave. It had grown late, and the maneuver guests were supposed to set out at dawn the next day. My departure, too, was right around the corner. And now suddenly a deep, enigmatic grief seized me, as though I were touched by the shadow of something irretrievably lost, something over and gone. I stood helpless in the face of its namelessness, for the farewell to the happy maneuver days did not seem to explain it at all. Perhaps—no, probably—it resulted from the knowledge that my parents wanted to send me abroad soon for a lengthy period of time, and, therefore, I would not see Golzow again in the foreseeable future as I had done every summer.

In reality, I never saw Golzow again. Already in the following year, the First World War broke out. My uncle died. Golzow was administered for a while, because Hans-Jeskow was still too young to take possession of the property—the manor, once so hospitable, stood empty for several years. Barbara married. My own choice of career led me to Southern Germany. And then came those terrible years in which the caricature of power appeared over our Fatherland. What my youth had experienced only as restrained might fell into the hands of criminals. Hans-Jeskow came into conflict with them early on. They spied on our correspondence; Barbara advised against any visit to Golzow.

Only after many, many years did I see her and Hans-Jeskow again—as impoverished refugees, as homeless as the dead in the Melliner Cemetery, whose fate had once shocked the sleepy little girl like a deadly premonition. The Second World War had also raged over us, a hurricane leveling cities and countries. Something that my uncle and the splendid officers who had been gathered on that last evening in Golzow would never have thought possible had happened: Germany, bleeding from a thousand wounds, lay prostrate, torn into two pieces. Prussia was declared dead; Golzow was lost. But something else had happened that I, at least, had never thought possible. We met initially in Munich, where I had driven to meet

Barbara and Hans-Jeskow. I must honestly confess that I had been somewhat anxious about this reunion: the Golzowians outside of Golzow—that had always been a not very happy notion, and now it was unspeakably painful. For these people had not only been ripped out of their very own world, but their world itself had met its demise; an entire land had been plowed up like that flowering lupin field I had once lamented. Yes, I was apprehensive about this reunion, but then everything happened very differently from what I expected. We did not speak of Golzow at all.

"Our children and grandchildren are safe and sound, as are we," Barbara said, waving off my concern with an improbably sunny smile, "and we are all healthy and able to work." Then she asked various questions about me and how I was doing. Hans-Jeskow, who had kissed my hand with the consummate chivalry of the old school, referred jokingly again and again to the fact that I had been his first love. He had come to look very much like his father and was therefore immediately familiar to me. I was unable to place Barbara, on the other hand, among the Golzowian faces that I knew. I would not have recognized her at all—she must have inherited the features of some long-since forgotten ancestor. The little Brandenburger bacchante of the maneuver days with the unspeakably naïve little face—how disturbingly shrewd and somber life had made her! Both she and Hans-Jeskow were in great spirits—I was almost ashamed of having feared this reunion. But I had probably been too young at that time to have been able to guess all the potential of these brave people. Instinctively I recalled the conclusion of the Prussian national anthem, as it had been belted out on my last Golzowian evening in the peaceful night of the trustfully resting countryside:

Sei's trüber Tag, sei's heitrer Sonnenschein. . . .

[Whether the day be cloudy or full of cheerful sunshine. . . .]

No, conquered Prussia was not dead, it was only changed —at that moment it stood before me, reborn to a new, inner fortitude.

Only as we sat at tea some days later in my own small apartment in the mountains did we finally come to speak of the lost Golzow.

"We were all gathered there once again when the catastrophe overtook us", Barbara recounted. "Hans-Jeskow had brought the whole family to the country estate when things got serious in the cities with the bombings. But then the deadly threat came to the countryside, too, in a different way, but no less terrible than in the cities. But you know, of course, that we had been forbidden to flee —we will not go into the details. So it seemed that there was no escape for us, for when we were finally allowed to flee, it was much too late. And yet we escaped at the very last moment, and do you know how? Through the marsh over the old Swedish footpath on which Anna Elisabeth had led the young cornet. We thought of her all during our flight and comforted ourselves with the thought that she was invisibly leading us, yes, as though the young Swede had already been thinking of us during his parting wish. We were quite calm, not even one of the little grandchildren cried—it was as though we were safe in the middle of the disaster. Do you understand that?"

I did understand it, but who would ever have thought that of the Golzowians! She turned a bit red; it looked strangely young with her gray hair—I was suddenly convinced that she was capable of tackling all of life all over again.

"You are surprised at us," she said candidly, "but Hans-Jeskow and I think very differently of Anna Elisabeth today than we used to. She, too, belonged to us, and although we disowned her, she remained faithful to us. For she, too, was a true child of our homeland and part of its strength—that feminine-maternal strength that the proud history of the world tends to remember only reluctantly and yet is deeply fundamental to every people: the half of all being, the womb of life, its first awakening and its last continuation, the invincible . . ."

"Do you mean humanity in general?" I asked tentatively. She responded: "Yes, that is what I mean, for ultimately it all starts with motherhood, and, oh, how gruesome world history is that betrays it time and time again!" And now tears fell from her eyes, which had indeed seen far too many horrors.

For a while, none of us dared to speak. Finally, Hans-Jeskow said, "But humanity is nevertheless the only thing that can triumph over the dreadful legacy of world history, and that is why Anna Elisabeth's obliterated countenance finally outlasted all of our downfalls." He told then of how one of his old, loyal tenants had recently slipped over the border and brought him news from Golzow. The manor had been completely ransacked, the family portraits had been burned; no memento of the former owners remained. Anna Elisabeth no longer stands and waits at the threshold of the house, either, but she is often seen by the villagers as she walks through the interior of the empty rooms: the hidden mistress of the house, the only one who could not be driven out by the new rulers: the spirit of the other, the unconquerable Prussian.

The Last Meeting

WHEN THE HEAVILY VEILED Marquise had reached the middle of the nave, suddenly she could not keep walking. An inexpressible dread came over her—she felt the tender, majestic power of love that streamed from the tabernacle, but she knew that if she went even one step farther, this celestial power of love would crush her: as though paralyzed, she remained standing for a few seconds—then she made a resolute attempt to step past her own horror, so to speak. But now she became aware that her tense body was putting up an odd resistance, a movement that was completely unrelated to her otherwise so powerful will— and immediately she remembered the possessed woman of Loudun who in her day had been talked about so much. With a gesture of unspeakable horror, she hurled the wax candle, which she had intended to bring to the altar as a votive offering for the deliverance she had just experienced, into a pew to one side—and immediately afterward she was tempted to snatch the candle up again so as to break it into a thousand pieces. For the deliverance on account of which she had intended to offer this candle signified a deception, after all. Still trembling within her was the terrible conversation she had just gone through with the man over whom she had ruled for many years and who now had become her implacable judge—a judge

79

who had exempted her from every earthly tribunal; the Marquise felt that in reality she was not rescued but rather forlorn! And now the dread that her soul felt in front of the tabernacle took possession of the stern clarity of her extraordinary intellect—a conscious fear, which was much deeper and more terrible than the one she had still felt a few hours ago at the thought of the earthly judge, shook her from head to toe—it seemed to her as if now, having the assurance that she had escaped that one, she stood for the first time before the true and inescapable tribunal —or rather: that its judgment on her had already been passed. She heard herself saying clearly and distinctly the words: "I am damned, I am damned for eternity!"

But like the tensions in her body, the utterance of these words had no relation whatsoever to her will—her own voice appeared strange to her, as if it were imitating someone else's or as though the words were wrung from it against her will—again she had to think of the possessed woman of Loudun! A mad despair came over her—she realized that the condemnation she had uttered was a definitive one, that there was no more absolution for her, no Sacrament of Penance could restore her innocence to her; instead, access to it was denied her just like access to the altar—the mere thought of it caused her to feel that same horrifying physical resistance as before.

"I am damned," repeated the strange voice that had taken possession of her, "I am damned for all eternity!" It seemed to her as if she had to cling to a human being in order to escape the clutches of her demon. But this too, she knew, was denied her. The few confidants of her terrible secrets had been entombed forever by a royal arrest warrant in the very silent prisons of Vincennes. As far as this world was concerned, her secret had been snuffed out. But a human being who already lived beyond this world could and perhaps might still hear the cry of the only woman to whom they had done the great injustice of a pardon. But where was such a child of Adam to be found? Only one occurred to the Marquise.

Immediately afterward she realized that she was in the same church in which the fortune-tellers of Paris regularly met with their female clients—for a moment she thought she could smell the scent of a certain powder that they had slipped into her hands—then she resolutely turned around, hurried to the door of the church, and ordered the coachman of her carriage that was waiting outside to drive her to the cloister of the Discalced Carmelites.

It was already close to sunset when she reached her destination. The portress at the turn looked indignantly at the late, heavily veiled guest who asked to speak to Sister Louise of the Divine Mercy. The speakroom was already closed; she explained; no more visits would be accepted.

"That is just why I want this conversation", the Marquise retorted. "I would like to speak to the Reverend Sister without witnesses."

The cloistered nun at the turn felt a justifiable annoyance. "You know very well, Madame, that the Rule of the Order allows no exception", she said reproachfully.

"Yes, I know it," the Marquise replied, "but the business on which I come justifies the exception."

"What Lady, except Her Highness the Queen, our Protectress, could demand such an exception of this cloistered order?" the portress asked, while making a gesture as though to close the turn.

The Marquise, still agitated by the breathless craving to cling to another human being, summoned all the haughtiness she had at her disposal.

"Yes, what Lady except the Queen could dare to demand that?" she repeated—it was as if a note of triumph crept into her voice, mysterious and at the same time revealing a mystery. The nun at the door cringed—she had grasped who stood before her: only one woman in all Paris could speak like that! Thoroughly intimidated, incapable of saying a word, she led the veiled woman into the speakroom. Then she hurried off, first of all to inform the Prioress about the astonishing guest.

A few minutes later, Sister Louise of the Divine Mercy stood before her spiritual mother, who told her discreetly but in no uncertain terms that the rumor was going around Paris that the all-powerful favorite of the King had fallen. Apparently as one seeking consolation and help, she now demanded to see her former rival, whom she had insulted so often and so severely.

"And now, my daughter," the Reverend Mother concluded, "now go with God to help the unfortunate woman. Change the former triumph of your opponent into the triumph of the Divine Mercy Whose name you bear, and receive for this purpose the blessing of your spiritual mother—yes, receive from her for this conversation every freedom to assist your opponent, and deny her no consolation that could serve the salvation of her soul.

Forget all the wrongs she has done you—the great hour of justice that God intended to grant you has come. It will be the hour of your own triumph, for no revenge is nobler than to do good to one's enemy."

Meanwhile, the Marquise waited impatiently in the speakroom into which the Sister Portress had led her. The room, in keeping with the style of the Carmel, was bare and frugal. But a grille that ran across the entire width of it displayed the gracefully intertwining bars of excellent ironwork. A crucifix was the only decoration on the wall, and beneath it burned the quiet light of an Eternal Lamp. A faint scent of church incense that had wafted over from the nearby chapel hung in the cool, close air—no stronger than the delicate scent of roses that billows over a garden wall.

The Marquise sat down on one of the humble stools that were set up for visitors, but immediately jumped up again and walked restlessly back and forth in the room— it looked as though this cool air, slightly permeated with incense, took her breath away—this air of another world almost like the next. But this was the one she had insisted on going to see.

It took a while before the Carmelite nun appeared behind the grille. She entered noiselessly in sandals, her head slightly bent, her hands folded under the wide scapular, and her thick black veil covered her whole face, as the Rule of the Order commanded.

"Praised be Jesus Christ", said a soft, almost alarmingly gentle voice. The woman waiting on the other side of the grille—she had not lifted her veil, either—oddly enough did not answer—it was as though the greeting of the one whose presence she had craved suddenly struck her speechless. A deep silence ensued.

Even before a single word was spoken, an extraordinary change took place. The Carmelite, too, had apparently expected something else—she began to tremble—the hands folded under the scapular of her religious habit let go and fell limply to her sides. The veiled woman on the other side of the grille felt herself breathe a sigh of relief—it seemed to her as though, at the sight of those defenseless hands, her reason for coming—that horrible reason—disappeared; oh, it was dangerous to show those slender, trembling hands; it was dangerous to set eyes on them! Those hands had once trembled in exactly that way when their owner had been sentenced to adorn *her*, the radiant rival—the narrow cloister room suddenly seemed to open up: what had been believed before poured in and broke through the bars of the stern grille. The tears of a woman who was no longer loved sparkled, but also the diamonds of a triumphant woman—the Marquise felt it was easier to breathe, as though the reason for her coming there, the entire dreadful incident that had moved her to do so, abruptly fell away from her, so powerful was the memory that came over her at the sight of her former rival. Quite unexpectedly she was absolutely certain that she would never, never take upon herself the humiliation of making to her former rival the admission for the sake of which she had come in the first place!

Meanwhile, the defenseless hands of the Carmelite nun trembled more vehemently; oh, yes, it was dangerous to show those slender, helpless hands—at the sight of those hands, the evil spirit of the Marquise had always risen in the past: the Carmelite nun suddenly had the notion that the other woman had not come as a fallen woman begging for consolation and reconciliation, as her spiritual mother thought, but, rather, to celebrate once again her former triumph—no, not her former one but, rather, an altogether present one! And now the Marquise, too, raised her veil—the Carmelite nun saw the notorious face of her former rival, still beautiful as a gorgeous, all-too-gorgeous flower, scarcely touched by the traces of the years, with a confident smile of victory as before, when they had called her "La Glorieuse" at court.

"Do you still remember the one for whom you so often held up the mirror when you adorned her, Madame de La Vallière?" the unveiled woman asked. It was as though she fed on the other woman's astonishment, gulped this astonishment down like an intoxicating refreshment—just like before! No, nothing, nothing, nothing had passed away; nothing could ever pass away; everything remained inextinguishably present forever!

The Carmelite nun crossed her arms over her breast.

"How could I not recognize you, Madame de Montespan", she replied softly. "Time has not dared to touch your beautiful face. I would gladly hold the mirror up to this face as before, but surely you have not called on a cloistered nun for that—what then can I do for you? I have no other wish but to serve you."

There was a delicate superiority in the gentleness of these words, a superiority of which the nun was probably not aware for an instant, which however agitated the Marquise unspeakably. Oh, how well she still knew the inexplicable impassivity of this soul, who was nonetheless so sensitive and vulnerable! How clearly she recalled this face—peculiarly moving now that it was slightly faded and care-worn—which she had tried so often in vain to reduce to anger and tears.

Today again, she felt the irresistible desire to do so! And once again now things past burst into the room, words that had died away long since resounded again, as though they had become present forever—all the candles of the royal chambers seemed to blaze up to illuminate that merciless scene, which the Carmelite nun thought had been extinguished forever from her memory and yet for her proved to be unforgettable until the end of her days!

She again saw the Marquise in the King's bedroom, being disrobed by her; she saw herself handing her the lace-trimmed nightgown—she had wanted to flee before the King entered—and in vain her eyes had begged her rival for the favor of leaving her; the other woman forced her to remain until—yes, until the terrible moment when she no longer could even beg because of the pain and the shame. With eyes glazed by the torment she had looked at the King—for a few seconds it was as though his eyes tried to give her an answer. But the high-pitched voice of the Marquise had already cut off that answer.

"Do give Madame de La Vallière your little dog at least to pet", the trembling rival had heard her say. "Do give her also something that she can press to her heart."

Oh, the speaker had known very well how infamous that request was—but the King, too, had known it—he had blushed, his natural chivalry had rebelled, but then he had picked the little dog up off the floor after all and handed it to his former mistress, so profoundly, so abysmally he had already fallen under the influence of the Other Woman. And now, of course, the moment must have come when the desperate woman would have to hurl the little dog away! But nothing of the sort had happened: the Marquise had been able to test her power even to the ultimate triumph! It had been twofold: victory over her former rival and victory over her reluctant royal lover. She still remembered exactly how for a moment she had been numbed by the success of her words. But then she had caught sight again of the trembling hands of her rival: the latter had not hurled the innocent creature away; she had stroked the soft fur of the little dog. In vain the Marquise had sought in her face the flush of anger or a torrent of tears! Had this lack of anger and tears been one final act of pride, or did it signify that a desperate woman's pain had been numbed? She did not know; she only knew that she had never managed to reduce that pale woman to tears—would she succeed today? She felt that wherever she met her former rival, under whatever circumstances, her presence would always awaken in her the same wicked delight.

And now everything that had brought her to this place was forgotten; she felt only that it was unbearable to think that her rival might learn the terrible background of her visit!

"Yes, I have a request, Madame de La Vallière", she said quickly. "I wish to know what prompted you when you pressed the King's little dog to your heart? I have often wondered about it but have never found an answer."

It seemed to the Marquise as though a slight tremor went through the figure behind the grille—but then she heard again the perfectly calm voice: "I am no longer Madame de La Vallière, now I am only the poor Sister of the Divine Mercy—you may question only the latter, not the former, Madame de Montespan!"

"But I am not asking the latter", the Marquise interrupted her. "I am asking the former mistress of the King—what prompted you then, indeed, what prompted you in the first place to remain close to your rival—why did you not leave the court, why did you not spare yourself that defeat?"

Again it looked as though the Carmelite nun wanted to turn and flee. But now she spoke with an excruciating gesture: "O Madame de Montespan, how can you ask such questions? Did I not flee twice to the cloister in those days, only to be brought back by the King? You know very well that he desired my presence at court."

"I know, Madame de La Vallière", the Marquise interrupted her. "Your presence at court was supposed to deceive my husband about the King's relations with me. But did not this same royal request give you a welcome incentive to leave court? I mean, did it not give you an opportunity to expose me to my husband? Really, were you not tempted to cause me those difficulties?"

For the first time, a slight agitation shook the voice of the Carmelite nun. "But you surely must understand, Madame de Montespan, that the King's wish was my command. Did you not feel the same way?"

Her words struck the proud heart of the Marquise like a blow, and it reared up in protest. "No, I was not childish enough to rely, as you did, on the volatility of such feelings", she said haughtily—it was her last attempt to insult the other woman. The attempt failed.

"Well, in that case—then right now I can only pity you", Madame de La Vallière whispered.

The Marquise was startled: What was the meaning of this pity? Did the other woman perhaps already know about her fall? Had the rumors of Paris been so hasty? Had they not succeeded in hiding her terrible secret from the world?

"So you are enjoying your triumph, that you can pity me, Madame de La Vallière", she said challengingly.

"I enjoy no triumphs now," the nun replied calmly, "for me only the triumph of the Divine Mercy exists—I have ceased to belong to the world of which you speak."

"But what did you feel when you still belonged to that world," the Marquise insisted, "what did you feel when you were still young and craved life? What gave you then the strength to endure your defeat? I am not asking the penitent of today; I am asking the former mistress of the King."

"You are mistaken, Madame de Montespan", the nun replied. "The penitent to whom you refer stood before you then when the splendor of the world seemingly still held her in its embrace. My true penance was not in the cloister but in the world—the cloister is the place of peace and blessings. The sins we commit in the world are atoned for in the world and . . ." very softly: "also in the world's sight. My sin was public; therefore my penance, too, had to be a public one." She paused, then she again said very softly, but also very firmly: "You yourself,

Marquise, were the one who determined my penance—
God had chosen you to be His instrument. Through you
I suffered all the torments that I myself had caused the
Queen; it was God's justice that thwarted me through
you. Every humiliation you caused me was a blessing for
my soul that you, although unwittingly, made possible for
me. And when you thought you were insulting me the
most bitterly, you were in reality the one who was purify-
ing me. You yourself, Madame la Marquise, were God's
instrument for me—may what you did for me prove to
be a blessing for you also—may God have mercy on you,
as He had mercy on me!"

The Marquise had listened to the nun's words with
bated breath—she was overcome by the feeling that she
had come here for the sake of these words. She sensed
a deep, wonderful movement within her as though the
grace that she had thought was lost forever were trying
to incline to her again—it was a moment like one she
had occasionally experienced before, when the priest in
confession had absolved her of her sins, which were so
small then. Oh, once she, too, had been pious and faithful! Suddenly it appeared to the Marquise as though all
the unshakable gentleness and patience of her rival, by
which she had felt provoked to sin, were in reality a single offer of grace for her. And now all at once she was
confronted again quite clearly with the reason why she
had come here—this agonizing fear about the salvation
of her soul! But was it not already too late?

No, it was not too late—she only needed to cling to
the words of her rival that she had just heard. The com-
pelling feeling overwhelmed her: now you must seize the

grace—now or never—she heard inside her quite clearly this "now or never"—one must not keep grace waiting! And then all those moments stood in a row before her in which she along her sinister paths had heard the words: Save yourself, before it is too late, because there is a "Too late!" Now or never—now or never! She hesitated another moment, but that one moment was fatal—it had already gone beyond the utmost limit of the heavenly patience that was being offered to her—and the next moment the wicked desire reared up again in her to insult this heavenly patience of the other woman in which the divine patience was apparently pleased to conceal itself. And now she already felt she was crossing a boundary that no longer instilled fear in her but, rather, gave her an almost intoxicating satisfaction, as though finally she could now enjoy in great draughts what she had once enjoyed only imperfectly. Slowly, emphasizing every word with heartfelt triumph, she said: "Your penance, Madame de La Vallière, has cost me dearly: if I was the instrument of your pardon, then you are the instrument of my ruin. Because you have enjoyed the happiness of forgiveness, there is no forgiveness left for me. Have you never reflected that your presence at court would necessarily drive me to despair? But pious persons like you naturally do not think of such considerations—as you ought—after all, you are constantly occupied with the salvation of your own soul . . ."

The veiled woman behind the grille raised her hands defensively. "No, not so, Madame de Montespan, not so. Why should my pardon become your ruin? Is it not rather a consolation for you? You committed the same sins as

I did when you yielded to the King's passion: we were sisters on the path of sin, and we will also be sisters on the path of Divine Mercy."

"How do you know that the sin I committed was the same as yours?" the Marquise asked haughtily. "Ah, you have never understood my relationship with the King!"

"I did too understand it, Athénaïs", the Carmelite nun said calmly. "It was your marvelous beauty that won the victory over me—no one could look at you without delight." For a moment the Marquise gave in to the tribute that her former rival ungrudgingly paid to her beauty, but then an odd, almost mysterious expression came over her face—as though its owner felt an irresistible desire to horrify her interlocutor.

Slowly, emphasizing each word almost solemnly, she said: "No, Louise, it was not my beauty that conquered the King—but something quite different: Do you know what a Black Mass is?"

The Carmelite nun cringed—incapable of speaking a word, she pressed her hand to her heart.

"Good, you know what it is, Louise", de Montespan continued. "How could you not know it? The whole world is talking about the proceedings of the *Chambre ardente* that the King instituted in order to put a stop to the so-called 'wise women'. The name of La Voisin, the woman whom they arrested, is on everyone's lips.

"Everyone knows the little house on the outskirts of the city where one could have a reading of the Tarot cards or buy that dangerous powder that could cause love or death, whichever was desired. But I assure you, there is nothing sinister about this house, located there in its

pretty, well-tended garden. Inside the house, too, everything is neat and clean; the walls of the rooms are decorated with cheerful tapestries, indeed, even with a few
pious pictures—why not, since La Voisin, the occupant,
was an upright woman—no demonic lover, but an hon-
est, somewhat simple-minded husband stood at her side.
It was all conducted quite soberly as with any other business. The customer placed an order for the desired Black
Mass and stated the incantations, that is, the intentions,
for which the priest was supposed to offer it, the price
was reckoned and paid, and also the price for the requisite sacrifice, indeed, even for its baptism, for La Voisin
would not allow the killing of children who were not
baptized.

"You are horrified, Louise, but, my heavens, what did
death mean for those little creatures, most of them born
illegitimately—a slash, a gasp, and it was all over." The
Marquise stopped—was she the one who had just spoken? How did she happen to say that? Had she not decided
at the beginning of this conversation that she would not
reveal her terrible secret? Was someone there who had
squeezed the confession out of her against her will? And
who was it? It could be only one person—precisely the
one to whom these ghastly Masses were offered. She was
struck dumb, shaken by a sudden horror, but she could
not remain silent: the invisible Presence once again took
possession of her voice.

"Well, what do you say now, Madame de La Vallière",
she heard herself ask almost insolently. "What do you say
now? I mean, what do you think about the pardon that I
supposedly helped you to obtain? Just now you called me

God's instrument for you, but have you ever wondered also whose instrument you were in my case?"

The nun hesitated with her answer—it was as though she had not understood correctly what the other woman meant. Then suddenly her pure, beautiful deportment started to waver—it looked as though her figure were about to lose the ground under its feet and sink into the abyss of that terrible partnership of which her rival had accused her.

The Marquise observed with breathless suspense. No doubt, this was a human being startled out of a deep, seemingly inviolable peace—a consoled conscience had flared up into helpless horror; something to which a soul had clung unshakably was about to snap—truly, the Marquise could be satisfied with the effect of her statement!

But now this unearthly voice that did not obey her at all spoke up again: "Is it not so, Louise," this voice said, "is it not so that you did not think you would once again be part of a Black Mass?—My God, you were so indescribably guileless—you did everything you could to calm your conscience—indeed, this conscience was your idol! How you caressed it, look at the cushions you offered to it! Certainly, you tried even then to flee to the convent, but no doubt you knew the King would bring you back—did it never occur to you that this game would necessarily drive me to extremes?"

The nun was now trembling all over, but she still uttered not a word. Meanwhile, the Marquise continued: "Do you still remember that harrowing journey we had to make together with the Queen in the same coach? The curious people who crowded the roadsides impudently called us the 'Three Queens'. You, Louise, had been brought back from the convent shortly before by royal command. You seemed sad and troubled, and the good-natured Queen took it for genuine remorse and had pity on you—ah, that little insignificant woman, she fell for your alleged repentance just like everyone else!—And why not? The King had made it so easy for her—oh, he played his part well then, the Sun King!—Of course he did not take her tears seriously, but he made every effort to dry them! Every time he walked up to our coach with his magnificent, lordly deportment, he tossed one of his enchanting witticisms at you, he called you the luckily recaptured beautiful bird that he did not want to miss at his court. Those words were designed only to be repeated confidentially to my husband.—You know that Monsieur de Montespan had just reappeared in Paris at that time, tastelessly clothed in mourning, on account of the wife who for him was as good as dead. I knew that very well, and you knew it, too—oh, no, you did not let yourself be deceived like the little Queen! But this comedy of the past, this stray beam of a sun that had long since set, was still for you the matter of your life—there was no other matter for you! Do you finally understand now when I say: this alleged repentance of yours was in reality your final happiness.

"You remained at court, because you simply could not tear yourself away from being close to the King! Even when you had been abandoned by him, he still remained for you the fulfillment of your life! And was I supposed to have no fear of such happiness? Do you not understand that you, in the helplessness of your love, continued to be my rival?! It was after that journey then that I ordered the first Black Mass—it was your doing! Or do you think, perhaps, like everyone else, that seduction implies nothing but bad example? Ah, Madame de La Vallière, you are acquainted only with the little, everyday transgressions—real sin, great demonic sin is kindled at the sight of a virtue or a beauty that we do not possess!''

She faltered—had she herself not testified in these last words that her rival was innocent of the Black Mass? Had the Invisible One not just played a sophisticated, mean trick on her? If that was the case, de La Vallière seemed incapable of noticing her advantage.

That delicate woman—torn away from all her ideas about repentance and the salvation of her soul, from her whole flight into cloistered peace, indeed, from the very hope for grace—was aghast: for the first time her tormented heart rose up against her cruel rival.

"You drove me away from the King's love," she blurted out, "and you are driving me away from God's grace—go. Go away, Marquise, I cannot bear your presence any longer . . ."

De Montespan burst into brief, strident laughter. "You tell me to go, Louise," she heard herself say, "but whither? To hell, perhaps?—I thought you would offer me your place in heaven, after I lost mine through your fault."

"I have no place in heaven to offer", the Carmelite nun whispered. She quaked now, aghast and horrified—it seemed to her that someone was tearing a veil from her soul and pushing open a door to chambers within her that she had not known about, much less ever entered.

"O my God, my God," she gasped, "are there then sins

committed of which we know nothing but are nevertheless ours? Are there then within us mysterious rooms in which no one is alone anymore?"

For everything that her cruel rival asserted was correct —her remaining at court as the abandoned mistress had been no penance at all but, in fact, her final happiness— she had simply been unable to tear herself away from being close to the King; even when he had cruelly rejected her, he had remained the meaning and matter of her life —just as a precious vessel of rose oil still pours out its perfume when it has long since been shattered.

And now it was as if all the candles once again lit up the royal chamber—unforgettable words resounded in de La Vallière's ears—no, no, nothing had been forgotten, nothing could ever be forgotten.

No supposed repentance could abolish what had happened; everything remained valid and present until the end of the ages and right up to the judgment seat of the all-knowing God—in His presence, too, Louise de La Vallière would not be the purified penitent she had imagined herself to be but, rather, the woman who loved unchangeably albeit guiltily, yet still the lover. And now her last pious assurance collapsed: the awareness of her love, into which she had fled, snapped, because this boundless, changeless final happiness that no pain could shake had driven her rival to mortal sin, to those terrible conjuring Masses with which she had purchased the King's passion: the whole abyss of the apparently uninterrupted chain of events connecting herself with her rival's crime became visible.

It seemed to the Marquise that she heard perplexed

sobbing behind the nun's veil. Had she finally attained her goal? Had she succeeded in reducing her rival to tears? Yes, she had attained it—an insane craving to see it with her own eyes came over her. "Let me see your face, Louise", she blurted out. The next moment she regretted her wish—she dreaded the countenance of the tormented woman as though she would meet in it the reflection of her own despair. But the Carmelite nun had already lifted her veil—did she thereby obey the order of her prioress to fulfill her former rival's every wish, or was she overwhelmed by the desire to disarm her cruel opponent with the sight of her?

We do not know what occurred in the soul of Louise de La Vallière—we know only that she lifted the veil from her face—it was drenched with tears.

In the convent they later propagated the legend that Louise de La Vallière, faced with her rival's terrible accusation, tried to unite herself by a look at the crucifix hanging on the wall to the mystery of vicarious suffering, but this is a hasty and all-too-easy interpretation. In reality, Louise at that moment was utterly incapable of that union, for she was still defending herself against the unjust accusation of her rival, and yet—despite all the weakness and human imperfection—she presented a distant image of that mystery. The Marquise recognized it instantly.

She wanted to flee, as before from the tabernacle in the cathedral, but she could no longer do so: the one who previously had taken possession of her voice now took possession of her body once again: unable to move from the spot, her limbs rebelled in a terrible contortion.

Simultaneously the light of the Eternal Lamp began to flicker uneasily—a spiritual darkness imperceptible to the eye seemed to break into the room—again the thought of the possessed woman of Loudon dashed through the mind of the Marquise. Then suddenly she screamed and threw herself, as though hurled by an invisible fist, against the wrought-iron bars of the parlor grille.

"Save me, Louise," she panted, "save me, I am lost; in time and for eternity I am a damned woman!" She rattled at the bars of the grille as though she were trying to break them apart, she struck her forehead against them, so that her beautiful, now completely distorted countenance bled—she turned away in pain, which nevertheless had nothing to do with this external wound.

And this raises once again the question: What was going through the soul of Louise de La Vallière? We know only that she did not stretch out her hands to her despairing rival, as the pious convent legend maintains, in order to quiet the unfortunate woman's terrible convulsions; rather, the latter's hands grasped now at her. With the incredible strength of the possessed, Madame de Montespan managed to force them through the bars of the grille and to cling to the helpless hands of the nun.

Upon being touched, she let out a faint cry of horror, but now she felt the convulsive spasms of the other woman subside. And the unnerving confession of the Marquise followed.

"Oh, how I hated these hands," she stammered, "how I hated them! Even as they adorned me so patiently, even when they pressed the King's little dog to your heart, I hated them—and now these hands are my last hope!"

She spoke as though being pursued from one word to the next, as though the destination had already disappeared though it was important to reach it nevertheless. Then suddenly stopping, as though out of breath: "But no, they are not my last hope, they cannot be! Ah, Louise, you still do not know everything!

"Those Black Masses were not only meant to stir up Louis' passion—they were supposed to cause your death, too! Yes, I made an attempt on your life, Madame de La Vallière—but the devil did not oblige me as far as you were concerned. Yet La Voisin was well acquainted with the moods of His Majesty the Evil One—when he failed to work, she lent a helping hand—oh, she had marvelous recipes, and there are many high-ranking persons in Paris who had use for them.

"Do you remember a certain white powder that was allegedly sent to you from a physician when you fell ill soon after our journey together? Your chambermaid admitted to me in tears that you had refused it. The good woman thought you did not want to get well but, rather, wanted to die while close to your beloved King.

"Only your love saved you then.

"But to make an attempt on someone's life is in reality already murder, for everything that is prepared within us and with our hands is in reality already there—everything is already there long before it actually exists."

And now it was as though all the lights of the royal court that had blazed up went out again; a strange, ghostly brightness appeared, as though a flame had escaped from hell and was dancing with a demonic gleam through the pretty garden of that little house on the outskirts of the city of which the Marquise had spoken. It whirled through the cheerful rooms with the appealing tapestries and the pious pictures; it flashed like lightning over the sinister altars of the Black Masses and the clean, neat kitchen of the woman who concocted poisons—it wandered through the palaces of high-ranking women, over the secret staircases of sin; it danced mockingly through the streets of the respectable citizens of Paris, through which the maidservants of crime had carried their deadly cargo, and it made its way right up the steps to the royal throne.

The Marquise did not dare to look at the Carmelite nun, but her fears were mistaken: to Louise de La Vallière, the attempt on her own life was of only little importance. Suddenly, though, she started as though struck by lightning. "For God's sake, Athénaïs, does the King know about—about these terrible admissions?"

The Marquise looked at the Carmelite nun with a glance so dark as to be annihilating. "Yes, Louis knows everything", she said coldly. "My name was betrayed by the accused under torture; my maid was confronted with the witnesses, who recognized her as the messenger between me and La Voisin—the tribunal of the *Chambre ardente* was obliged to communicate these statements to the King."

No answer followed—de La Vallière trembled all over, for now for the first time she understood: the painful happiness of her staying at court had been purchased not only with the crime of her rival but also with an offense against the throne, with the terrible humiliation of her beloved King!

"And so Louis, too, had to make atonement for his sins against the Queen," she finally blurted out, "but what a terrible penance you imposed on him—you, the woman whom he exalted like no other, the mother of his children, whom he made legitimate sons and daughters of France! Oh, if you had really loved the King, if you had really loved him, those Black Masses would never have happened! For the devil had only the power that you granted to him: no Black Mass induced him; only your unloving heart won him over!"

De Montespan's hands were now lowered feebly; she looked at her rival with a glance of abysmal despair.

"Louise, why do you have pity on the King and not on me, too?" she whispered. "Am I not a thousand times more miserable than he? Ah, concern about the glory of the crown lifted him up over every pain! You should have seen him, the way he stood in front of me during our last conversation in his unapproachable judicial attitude of clemency, as though I had never lain in his arms! Oh, His Majesty's clemency is terrible when the crown is at stake! Certainly, for my sake he dissolved the tribunal; there was a mistrial. The accused, indeed, everyone who knew about the trial even incidentally, disappeared into safe custody; the official records were burned in the fireplace of the royal cabinet, for the First Lady at the court of the most Christian King of all cannot be a criminal! Indeed, His Majesty's clemency is relentless when the crown of France is at stake! Just as you, a rejected mistress, were once supposed to deceive my husband by staying at court, so too now my staying there is supposed to deceive the people and society despite possible rumors that could still trickle out. I am supposed to appear to be the woman I no longer am; I am supposed to play the role of the woman I was long ago, just as once in the wagon of the 'Three Queens' you still had to play the role of mistress, although she had been abandoned long since! But what was for you a final, enigmatic happiness was for me the ultimate torment, because indeed you are right: I never loved Louis, and he never loved me, either, but only desired me, for the devil can grant everything, but not love—again and again it was only the power that a Black Mass gave me. Oh, Louise, power is the real gift of the devil! And I became intoxicated with this power: I could take the liberty of showing the Queen no consideration, as you did—what did I care about her tears?—the Sun King, to whom half of Europe bowed, bowed to me! And yet, I swear to you, Louise, if I were still allowed to call God as my witness, He would corroborate that I envied you nothing so profoundly as your love . . ." She paused, then said something almost inaudible: "And I still envy you your love right now, because much will be forgiven you on account of it, but nothing will be forgiven me for all eternity."

And now once again it was as if invisible spiritual darkness broke into the room and wrapped in endless solitude the last narrow paths of thoughts that lead to one another. But de Montespan's voice was raised again, now completely shattered, as though a desperate cry for help were making its way through disconsolate loneliness: "Yes, I envied you your love, Louise, but its heavenly patience, too, was what drove me to you with one last hope—yet I was wrong: it was in vain that I tried to burden you with my guilt—only the Divine Mercy itself bore the guilt of others, and I have forfeited this Mercy forever—with human beings, though, there is no fellowship between sinners and the righteous." Her voice broke.

And now we no longer wonder: What was going on in the soul of Louise de La Vallière? For the pious convent legend was right about this now: Louise de La Vallière united herself with the *Mysterium Christi*, vicarious suffering, but not as she had been accustomed to do previously, recalling only her own, her conscious guilt— suddenly she no longer felt that horrible resistance to a foreign, involuntary guilt that was imposed on her violently, but it was as though she heard deep inside her these words: If a soul can no longer believe in the Divine Mercy, then man must undertake the Divine Mercy. But in order to do that, he must also be willing to help bear someone else's guilt.

And now it suddenly seemed to Louise de La Vallière that it did not matter at all whether or not she really shared in the guilt of her former rival—she knew only this: just as there was a universally binding mystery of redemption, so too there was a universally binding mystery of guilt, which in its ultimate depths overflowed all boundaries like a heavy, dark tide.

"No, Athénaïs, there is a fellowship between sinners and the righteous," she said, "for no one is righteous in the first place. If I share unwittingly in your guilt, then you too share unwittingly in my love, for then— then everything is held in common! This heart, which you envy me, belongs to you, too—for the rest of your life its love will accompany you. Let us remain sisters, Athénaïs."

Again the Marquise eyed the nun with a long, sinister look—then tears welled up in the dry eyes of her beautiful countenance, as though a late spring rain were pouring down on an already wilted garden.

Suddenly she sank without a sound to her knees before her formal rival and slowly, almost solemnly, pressed a kiss on the hands that she had once hated so bitterly. Then she stood up, drew her veil over her tear-streaked face, and silently went out with her head bowed low.

The Tower of Constance

Cordially dedicated to my dear
traveling companions in Aigues-
Mortes, Peter and Claude Schifferli

THE PRINCE OF BEAUVAU had arrived in Aigues-Mortes in a
very bad mood because his high-ranking benefactress, the
all-powerful Marquise, had not wanted to hear about any
additional postponement of his dreary journey this time.
Therefore he had set out for this small, God-forsaken
backwater where, tormented by mosquitoes from the
marsh and haunted by impressions of the almost ghostly
landscape along the journey, he had spent a sleepless night.
In the morning he had attended Mass most dutifully, and
now, accompanied by his chaplain, he prepared to call on
the infamous Tower of Constance, where the prisoners
were kept.

The Prince, as mentioned before, was in a very bad
mood because he possessed a natural aversion to the sight
of human misery; hitherto he had succeeded to a great
extent in avoiding such impressions. But the Marquise
had pointed out to him the fact that his new office as
Governor of the district required him to undergo this
unpleasantness. "Follow my lead, dear friend, as long as
I can still advise you", she had insisted; "You will not
regret it." What did this strange word "still" mean? Did
his friend fear that she might lose her tender dominion

over the heart of the King? The Prince could not imagine that, yet he did not understand at all why the zealous patroness of Voltaire should make this clerical concern her own—nevertheless, the fact that she did was an indication: therefore he had complied with her advice, albeit reluctantly.

It was a dreary day full of silver-gray melancholy. The sea, which formerly had surged up to the walls of the city, had retreated. The harbor had silted up: where once Saint Louis' fleet of Crusaders had set sail while singing psalms, a pallid marsh landscape now extended as far as the eye could see; gleaming all over this reedy wilderness of grass were white crystals that the salt water had left behind in its flight, which now lent to the whole landscape a barren, spooky character. Did the sea, following the changing times, wish to detach itself, too, from its own proud past? Was it retreating mournfully from this place as the great destinies had done? The Prince did not consider this question as he listened, slightly bored, to the remarks of his chaplain, who in a courteous undertone called attention to the fact that previously in Aigues-Mortes the Albigensians and the Knights Templar had been imprisoned —therefore, if one keeps the Huguenots here, one is still walking in the footsteps of Saint Louis, for the eradication of heresy is the legitimate continuation of the Crusades.

Only with difficulty did the Prince suppress an impatient gesture, because he, like everyone in Paris with any education, was a staunch freethinker: he waxed enthusiastic about reason and freedom of thought, about nature and fine humanity. He had no dealings whatsoever with the concept of heresy: apparently in the days of the great Huguenot clans, it had been the path to power and influence, just as today one obviously acquired power and influence if you opposed it.

Meanwhile, they had come close to the Tower of Constance. Its steep, windowless walls stretched frighteningly high into the calm, pale silver sky, as though it had deliberately wrenched itself loose from the distorted landscape to get a view of the unruly sea. Had this tower, as its name maintained, not gone along with the changing times, and was the chaplain therefore right when he maintained that its present-day purpose confirmed the lofty spirit of the Crusades—the spire of this tower still sheltered the shrine of Saint Louis, did it not?

With their footsteps echoing, they now walked over the bridge of a musty, placid moat that ran around the tower. It smelled of seaweed and rotten fish—although this tower greeted the unruly sea from its height, its foundations were nevertheless set deep in the marshy ground of this accursed landscape.

At the other end of the bridge, the new arrivals were greeted by the still youthful commandant of the tower, who shortly before had succeeded his deceased father in that office. He handed the Prince the list of the prisoners; it consisted entirely of women's names. "The men are on the galleys", the young commandant explained. "Only very seldom do we get any who are too feeble for that service."

The Prince scanned the long list of names; beside some of them, a cross indicated that the bearer of the name had already died.

"How long are the prison sentences of these persons?" he asked. The young commandant looked at him in surprise—did the Prince not know that the years had been forgotten here?

"We have had no orders about that, my Lord", he said. "We hope to receive instructions from you", he added almost shyly, while his soft, still almost boyish face manifested a sympathy that he nonetheless dared not express —it was dangerous to take the side of the imprisoned.

The Prince understood the appeal that was being addressed to him. "That will depend", he said, "on the reception my chaplain meets with. He is commissioned to speak to the prisoners—I myself do not wish to come into contact with them: in no case will we have inmates falling on their knees and making stormy requests for clemency; refrain from speaking at all to me about such things." The young commandant bowed without a word —he had already noticed that the Prince in his attire had dispensed with all insignia of his rank.

Now they climbed a narrow spiral staircase. On that endless series of steps, the Prince imagined that he was inside a gigantic conch shell spewed up by the sea, whose ever narrower turns threatened to crush him to death. At the same time, however, he wished that the staircase would never come to an end, so oppressed did he feel at the thought of the sight that awaited him beyond it. But the moment he dreaded was already here. The young commandant opened the heavy door, which was secured in several ways, and they stepped into a large, round room; windowless and equipped with only a few narrow light shafts, it seemed at first almost dark. Musty, unspeakably stuffy, and stale air hit the new arrivals in the face. The Prince, accustomed to the fine perfumes at court, thought he would suffocate. Only gradually, as he became accustomed to the gloom, did he recognize a small group of women crowded close together and dressed in outmoded, faded garments; their faces were likewise colorless and faded, as though they were among the survivors of an era that had long since vanished, or rather its living dead. Instinctively he thought of the marine sediments: had bitter, salty tears accomplished here a work like the one performed outside on the landscape by the retreating sea?

The young commandant introduced "the prisoners", whereby he mentioned the name and age of each woman; there were many among them over sixty years of age, but, judging by their appearance, the Prince would have assigned a much higher age to almost all of them.

Meanwhile, the chaplain addressed to the prisoners the question: Were they willing to renounce their heresy and to return to the bosom of the Church? The prisoners remained silent. It was uncertain whether they were capable at all of absorbing the meaning of these words. The chaplain repeated his question, but, instead of the bosom of the Church, he inadvertently said freedom.

At first, profound silence followed again. Suddenly, though, two of these miserable figures held hands, as though trying to encourage one another: absurd, giddy, indeed, almost insane joy distorted their grief-stricken faces. Hand in hand they rushed toward the chaplain, but before they could utter a word, a cry resounded out of the background from a very feeble yet very clear voice: "Résistez!" The two women stopped and burst into tears.

The chaplain furrowed his brow: this resistance was familiar enough. "Whose voice is that?" he asked reluctantly. The commandant mentioned the name Marie Durand. "She is lying there sick", he added by way of an excuse. "No doubt she is talking feverishly."

"Nevertheless, she seems to be the soul of the resistance here", the chaplain replied.

The youthful face of the commandant showed growing uneasiness. "There are two sides to this resistance, Reverend Sir", he said. "Marie Durand possesses a wonderful knack for consoling the prisoners; in particular, she often keeps the new arrivals from despairing—my God, you have no idea"—in his agitation he spoke rapidly—"you have no idea how terrible these outbreaks are—please consider—please consider . . ."

"Well, then, lead us to your protégée", the chaplain interrupted him. "I am obliged to carry out my mission here."

They entered a niche of the room in which it was even darker and stuffier than in the main hall. On a frayed straw mattress lay an obviously very sick old woman. If the misery that the Prince had seen so far had been capable of intensification, it confronted him here—now he suddenly lost his composure.

"My God, my God", he murmured, burying his face in his hands; "How is it even possible to live here! What a disgrace for humanity!"

Meanwhile, the chaplain asked the sick woman whether

she had called out the word "Résistez". But now something altogether unexpected happened. The sick woman sat up and, without paying attention to the chaplain's question, stretched out her shriveled hand to the Prince. "Welcome", she said as before with a weak but nevertheless very clear voice. "Welcome, and fear nothing— it is good to be here."

Her words seemed to come from another world and were at first utterly incomprehensible; there was no response to them. And no one will ever be able to explain thoroughly what prompted Marie Durand to say them. Did she take the Prince for a newly interned prisoner, one of the men who had been sent back from the galleys, or was she merely trying to dispel his horror at her own misery? Did she think she had to console him about it, as she had already consoled so many? One thing only is certain, that this pitiful woman took pity on him.

"No, do not doubt", she continued. "Many have already come here in despair, but not one has remained entirely without consolation. For God loves the imprisoned—He gives them their interior freedom. He will also grant you yours. Oh, interior freedom is invincible—no tower, no door, however heavily locked, can do away with it."

The Prince, meanwhile, stood as though paralyzed. He felt something like a complete rearrangement of his whole world to date. Then suddenly he had the notion that he was standing at the top of this tower and seeing the ocean . . . "How long now have you been here?" he finally said.

"I do not know," she said pleasantly, "the time has passed so quickly—it has no importance here, almost

as though it were dead. . . . In this tower, eternity begins . . . ", she smiled.

"Marie Durand has been here for thirty-nine years",
the young commandant interrupted, drawing hope from
the Prince's shock. "She was quite young when they
brought her here; my father told me the story. She was
still almost a child, fresh and rosy as a little apple, so my
father described her—yes, as I said, that was thirty-nine
years ago now . . ."

"Thirty-nine years—thirty-nine years . . .", the Prince
repeated. As he did so his face changed, as though its pal-
lor matched that of the prisoner.

"Are you bidding us to leave?" the commandant asked
—he thought that the Prince had been overcome with a
physical weakness.

The man he had addressed gave no reply. Suddenly
he bent over old woman's shriveled, neglected hand and
kissed it reverently. "Marie Durand, you are free", he
said. "You are free this moment." Then, turning to the
young commandant: "They are all free—all of them; I
command you to release them today." He rushed out of
the hall and down the steps.

Not until he was down below on the bridge did the
chaplain catch up with him. "For God's sake, Your Highness, allow me to support you", he said. "Indeed, you
can scarcely stand!"

"On the contrary," the Prince replied, "I have just
gained a firm standpoint—I have lost my faith."

The chaplain was startled. "So you had a faith to lose,
Your Highness", he said with a touch of irony. "I was
unaware of that."

"Yes, indeed, I had a faith to lose", the Prince retorted. "I believed in the victory of atheism." The chaplain was taken aback for a moment. Then he said smoothly: "Very well, Your Highness, God's ways with a soul are often miraculous, but for now let us stay with men's ways. You were so gracious as to order the immediate release of the prisoners; the commandant requests of you the royal mandate necessary for that."

At that the Prince cringed: only now did he realize that he had overstepped his own delegated authority— the pardon of prisoners was the exclusive prerogative of the King. But under no circumstances could the command he had just issued be revoked; the inviolability of his authority as Governor was at stake.

"The commandant should attend to my orders", he said, not without a tinge of arrogance. "The royal mandate is my business; it will be produced at the proper time." And when the chaplain hesitated, he added: "The commandant has my word of honor as a gentleman."

A few hours later, the Prince found himself on the way to Paris, alone—the chaplain was following him in a second coach: the Prince, who was still deeply upset by his experience with the prisoners, could not bear any company. Moreover, he felt slightly unsettled at the thought of the royal mandate that he had to obtain immediately, for he knew His Majesty's reluctance to grant hasty audiences, he knew the countless antechambers in which one had to lobby if one wanted to reach the King's ear, and of course no time remained for that—the Prince intended to keep his word in any case, however difficult it may seem.

"Reinette will know what to do", he consoled himself —inadvertently he referred to the Marquise, his high-ranking patroness, by the little nickname she had had even as a young girl and which later proved to be a sort of prophecy. For Reinette had in fact become a little queen, or, rather, she was actually a great queen, for what significance did the ruler's wife have beside his all-powerful mistress? A shadow, nothing, the bearer of a mere title! Certainly, the path of this ascent had mortified the Prince at first: it had not been easy to relinquish his beloved wife to the King. Sometimes he had felt tempted to assume the role of the Marquis de Montespan, who once at the court of the Sun King had appeared in mourning garb when the latter had elevated the Marquis' wife to be his mistress. However, he had not appeared in mourning garb—times had changed: today, the important families considered it an honor to supply royal mistresses. Indeed, everyone was a child of his age, and one had to affirm it if one did not want to make oneself ridiculous. And Reinette herself knew how to console the Prince: her delicate hand and her cool intellect had been able to apply a plaster to his wounded pride. "Now I will finally be able to take care of you", she had said. "Now you will no longer be the inconsequential bearer of your great name; you will reach the place that befits you, and this, yes, this will be my real happiness at the King's side." And she had kept her word: as Reinette's protégé, he had climbed the steep ladder of success to the high office he held today. He had consented to this without resistance; indeed, a remarkable agreement had emerged between himself and Reinette, an agreement to which he had hitherto given no name. Today for the first time, a slight uneasiness surfaced, as though the wrong cards had somehow been played. But, of course, this worry resulted only from the excessive urgency of his concern.

Dawn was graying as the Prince arrived in Paris after a hasty journey; he had become accustomed, even as Governor of a remote district, to reside in the capital; indeed, he maintained in all seriousness that he could not live anywhere else. While en route, he had sent by mounted courier a note to the Marquise to prepare her for his request. He quickly shook off the dust from the journey, changed his clothes, and went without delay to Versailles to meet his friend while she was still at her *lever*, or rising, the alluring scene every morning that gathered together numerous followers of the powerful favorite. The Prince could hardly expect to enter her apartments. Now, on the threshold of them, when he was met by the delicate perfume of his friend, which otherwise usually enchanted him, he suddenly felt again this extraordinarily strong uneasiness. He hesitated for a moment to step closer, but the manservant had already thrown open the doors for the well-known guest.

The Marquise sat in front of her vanity table, having her hair done. She wore a costly, low-cut negligee that also left her shapely arms free. Since it was a dreary day, candles had been lit; they poured their warm, golden light over the whole room, which was filled with people. They thronged around the celebrated woman, some of them impatiently, some of them fondly languishing. A few were striving to hand hairpins to her chambermaid, so as to have the honor of having helped with the all-powerful woman's coiffure. Others, standing more in the background, held in their hands solicitation letters and were waiting for a gesture from the Marquise allowing them to deliver them. But she seemed entirely occupied by her personal adornment. With her gaze directed toward the large, ebony-framed mirror that her kneeling chambermaid held up for her, she smiled at her own image, while paying no further attention to the guests who had appeared at her *lever*. At first she did not notice the Prince, either, who, still battling with that peculiar uneasiness, had remained standing near the entrance. Although the Marquise was surrounded by all sorts of devoted admirers, an odd image occurred to him that had fleetingly intruded on his thoughts several times before at the sight of her: the image of one of those beautiful, shimmering snakes that are said to dance alone complacently in the moonlight. But this image was of course a deception, inasmuch as the Marquise in fact was not alone at all, and yet it must have some basis in reality.

Meanwhile, one could hear the voice of the lackey who had opened the doors for the Prince announcing the name of the new arrival. The Marquise turned her glance, and joyful astonishment glided over her face. "Well, then, welcome back, my Prince", she exclaimed, stretching out both her hands—very small, remarkably strong hands— but before the man addressed in this way could bow over them, her face underwent a change: the joyful smile vanished; the eyes—very intelligent, very alert eyes—looked at the Prince with surprise, indeed, almost with indignant fear. He suddenly had the notion that she shared his uneasiness or perceived it in some enigmatic way. But that lasted only a few seconds, and right afterward the Marquise again had control over her joyful, lively smile.

"I hail your return, dear Prince," she said with her unique, indescribably confident grace, "but I see this journey has worn you out . . ." Again her glance assumed the expression of faint amazement. Suddenly she stood up and said: "The *lever* is over; I thank my visitors. Until we meet again tomorrow morning", whereupon all present with the exception of the Prince withdrew. The desired moment had come: he stood before his protectress without witnesses.

She looked at him anxiously. "Poor friend," she said once again, "how this journey has worn you out! But it was truly necessary in order to improve your position in certain circles. As a freethinker you are accustomed to pay no attention to these circles, but believe me, they are very influential! And now let us speak no more about this journey", she continued cheerfully, "and, instead, see what a joy has been bestowed upon me!" She took out of a small display case an intricately carved ivory crucifix and handed it to the Prince. "A present with which the Reverend Mother Prioress of Saint Cyr honored me", she said. "As you see, my position with respect to certain circles has improved, too."

The Prince already knew about the Marquise's latest inclination to occupy herself with the sphere of piety. One found her reading devotional books; she collected pictures of saints and visited nuns. The Prince knew that she was hoping to receive absolution, which for years had been denied her as the royal mistress. But what did she need that for? Was she not an inveterate admirer of

Voltaire? What could the Church's absolution mean to her? Well, now, she just wanted to be victorious everywhere, the Prince had said to himself with an indulgent smile, one more small, perhaps endearing vanity, a gesture aimed at the goal of appearing at the communion rail as the pious woman whose ecclesial recognition not even adultery could damage—so the Prince had smiled previously at the religious efforts of his friend. Today he was quite alarmed when her little hand, adorned with precious rings, showed him the crucifix. Involuntarily he avoided her glance: quite suddenly he had before him the image of Marie Durand—how differently the crucifix would look in her hand! For a moment the conversation stalled, then the Prince regained his composure, for he was here, after all, in order to request the urgent audience with the King. Had the Marquise not received his note? Abruptly, without any preparation, he said, "Reinette, please give me an answer: Were you able to prepare my audience with His Majesty?"

The intelligent eyes of the beautiful woman became inscrutable. "And for what purpose, my friend, do you need this speedy interview?" she said casually.

Suddenly he had the impression that she already knew what impelled him to make his request. But how was this possible? Could she see in him his experience in Aigues-Mortes? Did she not only sense the change in their relations but also possess the explanation for it? Again his experience in Aigues-Mortes came to mind so vividly that he was convinced that she must detect it by looking at him.

Meanwhile, she shook her head with its finely powdered hair. No, she did not know at all, but she was accustomed to looking realities in the eye. Despite her apparent confidence, he clearly sensed her increasing alertness. Oh, she knew him too well, there was no point concealing himself from her.

"Reinette," he said helplessly, "stand by me, I must speak to the King immediately."

The intelligent eyes looked ever more guardedly, while her mouth continued to smile, not a forced smile at all: it was extremely easy for her to control her highly painted lips. No doubt it was clear to her that a change was at hand, and she sought the reason for it. "Did you do something stupid in Aigues-Mortes, my friend?" she asked in an attempt to joke. No, there was really no point concealing oneself from her!

"On the contrary," he replied vehemently, "I did the only sensible thing that could be done there: I gave the order to release the unfortunate prisoners instantly, but I did not have the requisite royal mandate to do so."

For a few seconds a profound silence set in. The Prince had the impression that the Marquise paled under the thickly applied cosmetics. Then she burst out laughing briefly: "Indeed, do you want to go to the prison in Aigues-Mortes yourself?"

And he tried to smile, because what she implied was after all utter nonsense!

"I must simply protect the young commandant", he said, without addressing her question. "I gave him my word as a nobleman that he would receive the royal mandate at the proper time."

Again the Marquise moved her fine head back and

forth, this time disapprovingly. "So you want to ask of His Majesty permission for the release of the prisoners that you have already taken in hand", she said. "Indeed, do you understand clearly what that means?"

"Reinette, I understand clearly that you can obtain anything from His Majesty", he said. Now she laughed quietly again. "Certainly, my friend, but you forget that I myself am seriously interested in obtaining absolution. At the moment I cannot possibly intercede with His Majesty for the pardon of heretics."

He felt now an insurmountable aversion to her religious efforts. Quite abruptly the image of Marie Durand stood before him again. And now two kinds of piety faced each other in the harshest contrast imaginable: there the sacrifice of silent, almost cheerful resignation to the lack of that ecclesial consolation, here the ambitious demand of a vain woman who hoped to gain religious recognition as though it were some stylish piece of jewelry. For a moment the Prince felt overcome by the desire to dispense with the mediation of his friend. But he could not afford such a dispensation, because his petition was too urgent!

"Reinette," he said anxiously, "if you do not help me, then my young subordinate is lost . . . You cannot force me to break my word of honor!"

Meanwhile, the Marquise had recovered from her alarm. "Calm yourself, my Prince", she said. "At this moment I cannot arrange the royal audience, but go on my behalf to Father Laroche and tell him frankly what happened in Aigues-Mortes. If anyone can settle your business with the King, he can. Hurry, before things become known!"

So he went to see the priest, who welcomed him with urbane politeness, without visible surprise. The Prince handed him a note that the Marquise had given to him as proof of identity—the priest broke the seal and read in an undertone: "Filled with deep concern about the preservation of our holy faith and extremely happy to be able to perform a small service for the Holy Church . . ." The priest paused and burst into high-pitched laughter. "That is the Lady Marquise, yes, once again that is quite the Lady Marquise", he exclaimed, visibly amused—it was as though he were saying: There she goes again trying to lie to me! Then, after he had read to the end of the letter silently, he said: "You are indeed in a difficult situation, my Prince; could the Lady Marquise promise you nothing at all?"

"She promised me your help, nothing else", the Prince replied in an irritable tone.

Now a half-ironic, half-indulgent smile flitted across the priest's face. It was a still youthful face with bold but extraordinarily well-controlled features, so that, despite all the ostensible unaffectedness, it gave the impression of being almost inscrutable.

"Yes, the Lady Marquise, the Lady Marquise," he said with a sigh, "she cannot be dissuaded from her wishes, once she gets something into her head." Without any further explanation, the Prince became convinced that through the mission with which she had saddled him here, his patroness intended to expedite her own absolution by the priest and that the latter, too, had understood this quite well, although he wasted not a word on the subject—silently he folded up the Marquise's note. Then he said: "You feel drawn to the Protestant faith, my Prince, do you not?"

"No, on the contrary, I am a freethinker, but through the prisoners in Aigues-Mortes I have seen what it means to be a believer", the Prince replied. Although he was in very narrow straits, he felt irritated and was tempted to emphasize to the Jesuit the impressive attitude of the heretics.

The priest understood the challenge but kept his unshakable imperturbability. "And how did you word the command that you left behind in Aigues-Mortes?" he asked with objective determination.

The Prince felt a vehement impulse to ruffle the Jesuit's amiable politeness. "As Governor of the district I gave order to release the unfortunate prisoners immediately", he said haughtily—he enjoyed once again at that moment the triumph of his powerful position. But the priest did not do him the favor of being horrified, as the Marquise had done.

"Quite understandable, my Prince," he said benevolently, "quite understandable from the perspective of humanity; I understand you completely." Then with a subtle smile: "We Jesuits, too, have observed the latest intellectual developments, which in the long run are not entirely without advantage. This rationalism, however disastrous its effects on religion may be, had to come —religion alone could not cope with fanaticism."

The Prince's amazement deepened into astonishment; meanwhile, the priest continued candidly: "Therefore, I completely respect the order that you gave in Aigues-

Mortes, my Prince; but of course it could not be carried out, since it lacked the royal mandate."

"But it was carried out", the Prince said emphatically. He felt now increasing satisfaction in standing up for his unauthorized deed; again he savored the triumph of his position. "The young commandant carried out my order as a matter of course; he needed only my promise that he would receive the royal mandate later on."

"And you are certain that a royal audience will obtain this mandate for you after the fact?" the priest asked.

"Why not?" the prince replied obstinately. "The King is not a bigot . . ." He deliberately chose this word discrediting piety, but the priest indifferently overlooked this, too, and even repeated the word: "No, the King is not a bigot," he said, "but he is bound by certain religious duties: his coronation oath commands him to destroy heresy. You forget, Prince, that in this matter of the persecution of your charges, you are dealing less with the Church than with the power of the State, which desires a populace that thinks uniformly." He hesitated a moment, then continued: "As I already said, my Prince, you are in a difficult situation—I care less for the young commandant than for you yourself: after all, he followed the order of his superior, whereas you overstepped the command of yours. I fear that we must reckon with the possibility of legal proceedings against you."

At the priest's words, the Prince had the feeling that he was being pushed quite suddenly into the primordial darkness of a room with no exit whatsoever, whereas until then he had deliberately given no thought to its threatening presence. Since he had always been concerned only about his young subordinate, the intense awareness of his name and of his extraordinary position had lulled him into a sense of security. Now the Marquise's witticism, "Indeed, do you want to go to the prison in Aigues-Mortes yourself?" suddenly stood before him as a terrible possibility.

No, the Prince of Beauvau was not a heroic character; he was a fine aristocrat, accustomed to the discreet language of courtiers and the beautiful, sentimental ideals of its philosophers; he had constantly served no master but success and preferred the life of his privileged class to any, even the smallest, sacrifice. Faced with the prospect that the priest had indicated, he felt a horror similar to the one he had experienced when confronted with the misery of the prisoner Marie Durand, but now this horror pertained to the Prince himself and to his own fate! He knew that the possibility that the priest indicated had very definite precedents: had they not sentenced a number of noblemen a few years before because they had been found guilty of having listened to a Protestant sermon? And even though his social position protected him from the fate of the galley slaves, imprisonment for him was certain, perhaps in Vincennes, perhaps in Besançon, perhaps in that Tower of Constance! And he himself had had a presentiment of it the whole time but again and again had successfully repressed the soft stirring of the thought. Now his life, still unfurled right now in the courtly splendor of Versailles, seemed to be transformed into the melancholy landscape of Aigues-Mortes, which had horrified him from the first moment. He saw the landscape before him in its unbounded bleakness, covered with the salt of the frozen tears of the sea, which had incessantly fled from that shore and off into its own unattainable liberty! Going to the tower in Aigues-Mortes had indeed been stepping into another world from which there was no return.

The priest had not failed to notice the profound dismay of his interlocutor. "Nevertheless, it is of course advisable to inform the King," he continued, softening his tone, "and here it appears to me that the Lady Marquise is after all the only person qualified to present an appeal for royal clemency, not for the unfortunate prisoners— that unfortunately would be pointless—but rather for you yourself." He paused, because the Prince was shaking his head with an indescribable expression.

"I understand", the priest said. "You do not think that the Marquise is willing to help, and indeed she has other purposes in mind; I admit that this is an unfavorable moment for your request." He avoided becoming any clearer.

But the Prince had long since understood what it was about—he could no longer control his agitation. "Father," he blurted out hastily, "can you not give the Marquise absolution, so that her hands are free?"

The priest shook his head with an almost youthful movement: "If the Lady Marquise is willing to leave Versailles forever: yes," he said smiling, "otherwise, no. About morality we can debate just as little as about the faith. Meanwhile, precisely her absence here is for you, my Prince, an opportunity, I mean the prerequisite for a power that perhaps would be the only one capable of giving a milder interpretation to the coronation oath—

I repeat: of course for you alone, not for the prisoners. And if I am correctly informed, you have already been able to test this power several times."

He broke off, because plainly something unexpected was occurring in the Prince. "Is there by any chance some repugnance on your part to the help of the Lady Marquise?" he asked in dismay.

The Prince was silent for a few moments, then said with a strained voice: "Yes, I find it repugnant." What until now he had only dimly suspected had suddenly become absolute certainty: the shadow of Aigues-Mortes had reached his relationship to the Marquise! The unsettling feeling that had come over him fleetingly upon entering her chambers—no, already in the coach on the journey back to Paris—broke through into his consciousness with colossal clarity: he could, he should no longer ask this woman for her mediation.

The priest, who stood facing him with his eyes lowered, looked up at him with a quick, intelligent glance. "I understand," he said with keen insight, "your experience in Aigues-Mortes was not only upsetting, humanly speaking, but also transformed you interiorly: You prefer to entrust yourself to God . . ." He stopped, because the Prince suddenly buried his face in his hands: he felt helpless, at the mercy of a trial that was slowly but surely depriving him of all hope.

For a few minutes, silence reigned between the two men, then the Prince said: "No, that is precisely what I cannot do. In Aigues-Mortes I lost my faith in atheism. I discovered that Christian faith still exists, but I myself am far from that faith." Then with desperate determination:

"Therefore I must speak to the King—Father, is there no possibility of being saved by you, I mean by your Order?" The priest looked at the Prince with sincere sympathy. "I had better advise you to go abroad", he said, "and to do so immediately. The chaplain was present at the incident in Aigues-Mortes, and no one can blame him if he informs his ecclesiastical superiors, and then you yourself will know, Prince, what attitude our great French princes of the Church adopt toward those of other faiths, although almost all of them flirt with pagan philosophy. And yet these princes of the Church have long since ceased to be the ones to make the final decision—I think, Prince, that again and again you are mistaken about the real situation. We are dealing with the power of the State!"

Now the Prince no longer restrained himself: all the rumors circulating in society about an almost fabulous power of the Jesuit Order paved the way. "But what does the State matter," he exclaimed, "when the opinion of the powerful Order that you, Father, represent here is in favor of tolerance?!"

"Tolerance is not the opinion of my Order, which I represent here," the priest replied, "and it never will be. But neither is this about tolerance at all. Rather, it is about something subtler and deeper: it is about humanity and mercy, which one owes also to those whose faith one fights against. Nevertheless, the hour of mercy has not yet tolled in this country, but it will come, perhaps in a hundred, perhaps only in two or three hundred years— our conversation here . . .", he smiled, "is playing out, so to speak, in future centuries. Centuries will come when they will make the most serious accusation against us on account of your prisoners: all who on account of their faith are chained to the galleys are rowing the bark of Peter toward storms of indictment, although the Holy Father has told us that current methods are not Christ's and that we should lead those who are fallen away into the Church and not drag them in. But these Gallican free spirits do not feel obliged to heed this fatherly voice."

"But people say that your Order is so intelligent and powerful that it is capable of accomplishing anything", the Prince naïvely insisted, literally clinging now to his interlocutor.

"No, we can accomplish nothing at all," the priest replied, "not even the most modest moral order at the court of the Most Christian Monarch, as the case of the Lady Marquise with which we are dealing demonstrates. The truth is that we are endangered no less than you, my Prince . . ." He hesitated for an instant, then continued with a smile, "No, really, Prince, our position is not at all dissimilar to yours: there are serious intrigues against us, intrigues that go as far as Rome, in pursuit of the disbanding of our Order. I would not be at all surprised if we, too, had to leave this country soon."

Again the Prince's astonishment deepened into bewilderment. "So then you, too, are fighting a losing battle?" he said incredulously.

"That goes without saying—a Christian always fights a losing battle," the priest replied cheerfully, "and quite so it is in the Order, too: to fight a losing battle means to take a stand where Christ, too, stood here on earth. The matter becomes dangerous only when a Christian seizes the banner of this world in order to save himself."

The Prince looked helplessly at the priest. He did not understand his attitude. Did it spring from the famous holy indifference, the entirely disinterested equanimity toward all personal success or defeat that the Jesuit Order was said to cultivate?

"But the only thing I can do is to seize the banner of the world," the Prince exclaimed in desperation, "because this world is very, very dear to me—I have no other to lose!" He had reached the end of his composure. The priest looked at him with sincere apprehension. He mentally assessed the other man's available strength—the experienced observer of human nature saw that, by earthly standards, it was insufficient.

"Well, then," he said, "let us save the world, my Prince, but really, the only way is through the Lady Marquise: her power over the King is limitless; not he, but she is the real ruler of this country. Wait a moment . . ." He dashed off a few lines on a piece of paper, which he then handed to the Prince. And when the latter hesitated to accept it, he added with a smile: "There is no intrigue connected with these lines, as you evidently believe about the Jesuits. I am in the fortunate position of being able to assure the Lady Marquise quite simply that, contrary to her own opinion, she will perform a service to the Church if she endorses your request to the King—you understand: to the Church of the future."

The afternoon sun was already casting its slanted rays onto the streets of Paris when the Prince left the priest. He found himself in the most peculiar mood in the world. He still felt an extraordinary repugnance toward his friend.

Should he not try first with his philosophical friends: it was said, after all, that they had great influence on the high-ranking clergy, and was it not common knowledge, too, that Monsieur Voltaire had intervened for the rehabilitation of the unfortunate Huguenot Calon? Of course, Monsieur Voltaire was in England at the moment; meanwhile, should his friends not use the opportunity to help bring about the victory of their fine theories about humanity? The Prince decided to visit one of the famous salons where he customarily met with his philosophical friends.

And sure enough, he was in luck. "Charming of you to come, dear Prince", they greeted him. "You are credited with astonishing things: they maintain that in Aigues-Mortes you played the role of the hero of the Huguenot believers—we expected to see you again with a Bible in your hand."

The Prince reddened. "And I", he replied irritably, "expected that society, which you have converted to reason, would not believe such fables . . ."

They laughed. "We congratulate you on your optimism! Unfortunately, we ourselves have arrived at the conviction that reason is beautiful, although it is found so rarely. But we are surprised that this fact did not occur to you right in Aigues-Mortes. The fate of the prisoners there is sure proof of the absence of any reason whatsoever among our contemporaries."

"Proof, above all, of the absence of any humanity", the Prince replied. "Our mutual friend Monsieur Voltaire not only spoke but also acted along these lines. May I appeal to your humane help as well?"

At these last words of the Prince, a brief, embarrassed silence ensued. Then a somewhat disconcerted voice spoke up: "For God's sake, Prince, surely you do not mean to exhort us to patronize the measure you took in Aigues-Mortes? At the moment we have fallen into disfavor in court—they have had a book by Monsieur Voltaire burned by the executioner—No, at the moment . . ."

The Prince stood up. He felt quite clearly that these men could not save him and would not save him, for, indeed, he was no longer one of them at all! For the first time he was disappointed by the famous man, whose faith in reason was shaken because he saw that he himself had fallen into disfavor—what vanity! Was that still the same friend from years past, who used to take his mind for a stroll here in the aromatic café? And what did this mind matter in comparison with what he had experienced in Aigues-Mortes? What did a burned book matter as opposed to the sacrifice of an entire life? And now, after all, he had only the Lady Marquise left.

Therefore he went for the second time that day to Versailles, for, by God, there was no time to lose—Monsieur Voltaire had proved that to him, since he already had knowledge about his adventure in Aigues-Mortes.

Dusk was falling as his coach and horses stopped at the main entrance to the palace. It was remarkably quiet and dark there despite the still-early hour. The Prince learned that the meeting at the gaming table, which otherwise usually assembled the society at court at this time, had been cancelled and that the Lady Marquise had already withdrawn to her bedroom. He ordered the servant to announce him, nevertheless.

The maidservants were just undressing their Mistress as he entered. He had the disagreeable feeling that the Marquise was awaiting the King, a notion that filled him with intense uneasiness. At the same time, however, he felt also the perplexing enchantment of the room, whose intimate objects reminded him of those evenings when he himself had been awaited by his beloved wife. Over the gilded back of a chair, the chambermaid spread the silk nightgown of her mistress, then she fluffed the pillows on the bed; finally, obeying a gesture of the Marquise, she discreetly withdrew. How well the Prince knew this gesture, too, and with what trembling expectation he had once welcomed it! Today at this gesture, he was convulsed by a savage pain, which for a moment even numbed the fear that had driven him here.

Meanwhile his friend attentively read the lines that the priest had sent with him. As she did so, her features visibly brightened; evidently the Jesuit had found the right words. "Good, I will arrange the audience, Prince; you and the priest should be satisfied", she said with a very promising smile—plainly she thought that she had come closer to her destination. But strangely, this assurance did not relieve the Prince. "Reinette," he said uncertainly, "sometimes I am ashamed of your advocacy with the King. Can you understand that?"

"No, not at all", she replied with a gruffness that told him that she had guessed his thoughts. Her face, from which the chambermaid had removed the cosmetics, paled, so that the first traces of fading could be seen on it—they deeply moved him with wistful tenderness. And now a tempting idea came over him: he must cast off all the honors and goods that she had obtained for him. For was not earthly love, too, a gem that one ought never to sacrifice to outward success? The experience in Aigues-Mortes had therefore taken hold of this room of his life! An oppressive silence ensued.

Meanwhile, a little clock standing on the mantelpiece struck the hour with a childishly high-pitched sound— the Marquise's face assumed a listening expression: outside, steps were approaching, the door opened, and on the threshold appeared the King. Like the Marquise, he was in a nightgown, the loose folds of which showed his well-formed figure. A certain puffiness had settled on his still-handsome face; a slight softening of its features betrayed the all-too-sensual life of its owner. At the sight of the Prince, the astonished monarch stopped in mid-entrance, obviously unaccustomed to finding another visitor at this place and at this hour. Had the Marquise intended this encounter when she received her former devoted admirer? Was she yielding to the only opportunity to fulfill the priest's request? No doubt she was playing a risky game. For a few seconds, all present remained as though paralyzed; then the Marquise flew to the King, seized his hand, and pressed it tenderly to her heart.

"Sire," she said in a slightly faltering voice, "excuse the presence of the Prince of Beauvau; he is here in dire straits to beg a favor of you: be so gracious as to give him a hearing, I earnestly beg you."

The King's face showed awkward embarrassment. "How could I refuse something to such a petitioner?" he said hesitantly. Then, turning to the Prince: "Therefore speak; what do you request of me?" His voice was slightly restrained.

The desired audience was there, but the Prince was unable to make use of it. Had the meeting overtaken him too abruptly? He felt that his aversion to the mediation of the Marquise was becoming gigantic. He now had no doubt whatsoever that the King knew about his former relationship with Reinette; indeed, the overwhelming thought occurred to him that this knowledge was the secret of all his successes, the foundation of his incessant advancement—this advancement was, so to speak, the compensation that the King granted him for the loss of his beloved wife! And now once again everything fell under the shadow of Aigues-Mortes.

Meanwhile, the King was still waiting for his answer. The Marquise was already trembling all over. "Sire," she hastened to say, "allow me to make myself the Prince's advocate: the matter is a false step that your magnanimity will forgive him. The Prince was in Aigues-Mortes and released the Huguenot prisoners there; he begs of your great, benevolent heart authorization for it after the fact." As she spoke the last words she raised both hands, and the light covering slipped from her beautiful arms, and while she persisted in that graceful posture the Prince again had the impression of a shimmering snake that has reared up and begins its seductive dance in the moonlight.

As the Marquise spoke, the King had raised his boldly arched but somewhat too thick eyebrows, so that they climbed over his brow like thunderclouds. "I know, I know already", he said carelessly. "The chaplain of the

Prince dutifully gave the Lord Archbishop of Paris a report on the events in Aigues-Mortes. Proceedings will be
brought against you, Prince, because your conduct was
illegal in every respect. I regret that I can give you no
other advice than to leave France as quickly as possible.
I will make sure that you reach the borders unhindered.
Meanwhile, they can detain again the prisoners whom
you released, and as soon as that has happened, the matter will quickly be forgotten. In a few months you can
return to Paris, and now do not thank me, but rather the
Lady Marquise."

The last invitation struck the Prince as the expression of
a secret triumph over him of which the King was aware.
Again he remained silent—had he not understood the
King's words, those words that suddenly relieved all his
worries, guaranteed his safety, and banished the terrible
dread of imprisonment? He was to evade the coming trial,
then return in the foreseeable future, and everything was
to be again as it was before: he was to go in and out of
court, success and distinction were to accompany him
further, he was to participate in the receptions of high
society, sit in the evening at the gaming tables, dance the
festive gavottes, enjoy all the advantages of his high rank:
in short, this whole resplendent comedy of his life would
begin over again; he had only to stretch out his hands
for it!

But he could not stretch them out: very clearly he heard
a soft, feeble voice that whispered right at his ear the unforgettable word "Résistez." He knew that there was no
authority in the world that could command him to ignore
this word: it would pursue him for the rest of his life and

reappear whenever it was important not to surrender a great or the greatest good!

And now a marvelous thing happened: dread of impending imprisonment abruptly turned into dread of the pardon that the King was offering him. In astonishment, he realized that he had already crossed the border that separated him from his whole previous world, and now this world vanished definitively before his eyes, as a tall ship with its rigging sinks into the waves. An irresistible break with his entire past had taken place, a break that he had desperately resisted and that he now had to own nevertheless, for never, never could he abandon again the prisoners whom he had freed: indeed, their freedom was like his own.

Meanwhile, the face of the King, who was still waiting for his answer, assumed the expression of pained impatience—a mask was about to fall. "Why do you not give thanks to the Lady Marquise", he asked gruffly. "Perhaps you do not approve?" These last words sounded challenging, almost hostile.

"No, I do not approve, Sire", the Prince heard himself saying. It was as though language had become independent and, without the slightest effort of the speaker, was forming its statements out of his deepest interior necessity. "No, I do not approve, for I cannot allow pardon to be granted to me but not to the prisoners as well."

Once again the King controlled himself: "What does it mean, in regard to me, to say 'I cannot allow'? You know as well as I that the Edict of Nantes has been revoked."

"But not the law of humanity and of mercy." Again the Prince heard himself speak without his assistance.

The King's raised eyebrows collided, forming an almost horizontal line across his forehead—the threatening storm came up. "Do not forget, Prince, that you are speaking with the Most Christian King of France, who has to watch over the faith of this country", he said haughtily. "Who will guarantee for me that your liberated prisoners will not endanger this faith?"

"I guarantee it, Sire, I vouch for them", replied the Prince, or, rather, that unwaveringly independent voice that he nevertheless recognized again and again as his own. But now the King's voice, too, had something of an instinctive force: "How do you envisage this guarantee? Do you perhaps want to go to the tower in Aigues-Mortes instead of your prisoners?"

For the third time that day, the specter of the tower in Aigues-Mortes appeared to the mind's eye of the Prince as a personal threat. Did the revival of his inward freedom signify outward imprisonment? An oppressive silence ensued, then the Prince said softly but with extreme clarity: "Do not forget, Sire, that there is a freedom before which even the power of the King of France ends."

The King's voice became threatening: "I think, Prince, that it is better for you if we end this conversation." That was the unmistakable command to withdraw!

But the Prince did not go; he did not move from the spot. "Sire, I ask you for the prisoners' freedom", he repeated.

Suddenly it looked as though the king intended to abandon the majesty of his deportment. "Have you not noticed that the Lady Marquise and I wish to be alone?" he remarked imperiously to the Prince. "Really, what else do you wish?" And now something quite different from the fate of the prisoners was in the room.

The Prince froze. Then his anger blazed up high. "I wish, Sire," he said trembling, "that I had appeared before you in mourning garb as the Marquis de Montespan once did before your predecessor."

The King's countenance turned ashen, then his mortally wounded pride straightened up. "Do you remember also how long Monsieur de Montespan spent afterward in the Bastille?" he asked icily. "No, you do not remember—now you will have an opportunity to reflect on that." Then, turning to the Marquise: "I have heard, gracious Lady, that absolution is being denied you unless you leave Versailles—I place nothing in your way, if you want to return to where someone thinks he has a claim on you." Then he left the chamber without deigning to bid farewell to those present. When the door had closed behind him, the Marquise sank into an armchair and covered her face with her small, now very helpless hands. "This is the end," she gasped, "this is the end—oh, why did you speak about Monsieur de Montespan?!"

"I should have spoken about him years ago, Reinette", he said. "I should have helped you defend our love. But I did not help you. I took part in the undignified bargain —can you forgive me?" Involuntarily he reverted to the familiar form of address as in the past, yet she did not notice it but continued to lament: "Oh, that wretched journey to Aigues-Mortes! I felt the transformation the moment you returned—what happened to you there?"

"This is what happened, Reinette", he replied. "I saw there a human being who is sacrificing and enduring everything for the truth of her life, while we have sacrificed the truth of our lives for the goods of outward success and glory. But now that is over forever—do you not feel the liberation, too?"

"Liberation?" she repeated, "Liberation? Indeed, did you not understand what the King meant when he spoke to you about the Bastille?" She, too, now used the familiar form of address.

"Yes," he replied seriously, "yes, I understood it." As he said that, he realized with astonishment that his fear of imprisonment had disappeared.

She looked at him wide-eyed and uncomprehending. "The King will not spare you", she lamented; "I know him, he always hated you because he knows what there was between us—alas, everything he granted me for your sake sprang from that hatred, that constant feeling that he had to compensate you for ownership of me—he is too proud to take me away from another man. Now that he has dismissed me, he will no longer force himself to be considerate: you must be off, this very moment, if you want to reach the border in time."

"Yes, this very day I will set out for Aigues-Mortes", he replied calmly.

"For Aigues-Mortes", she cried in horror. "You intend to go to Aigues-Mortes! Do you not understand that you will thereby lose the little time you have left?"

"No, on the contrary," he replied, "I am conscious of making use of the last precious time."

She looked at him in speechless horror. Then her glance was transformed—an hour earlier this change would have intoxicated the Prince, but since then the world had changed. Suddenly she threw herself into his arms: "Do not abandon me, too!" she begged, "Deep down I always loved you alone after all!" He gently got away from her: "Reinette," he said, "where I am going I cannot take you with me—now I can only forgive you, as you must forgive me."

We are coming to the end of this incident, about which we can speak, however, only with restraint, for the circumstances of it have been variously interpreted, not to mention distorted. The Prince's journey resembled a flight: he used an inconspicuous vehicle; he had dispensed with all retinue; he ventured to travel only by night.

It was early morning, as in the case of his first visit, when he approached the infamous tower of Aigues-Mortes. Its menacing, uplifted head stood even gloomier and more repellent over the melancholy landscape than it had done back then. But this time the Prince felt a quiet sympathy along with the sadness. He was filled with an interior affiliation with it; he was willing to take it upon himself —so willing that it almost became a secret joy.

As he stepped onto the bridge that led over the dark waters to the entrance of the tower, he saw at the end of it a rural covered wagon. The commandant stood beside the driver, to whom he was evidently giving some instructions. When he caught sight of the Prince, he left the other man there and hurried to meet the new arrival.

"God be praised, my Prince, that you are bringing me the royal mandate in due time", he exclaimed. "Right now I am releasing Marie Durand, our last prisoner—I kept her back *pro forma*—I mean, so as to be able to say that I did not act without royal permission."

The Prince greeted the commandant but did not address his expectation of a royal mandate; instead, he asked to be taken to Marie Durand. They walked to the vehicle, and the commandant gestured to the driver to fold back the cover. "I had him spread it over the wagon because she can no longer endure the sunlight", he explained. "All the women whom we released were almost blinded after decades of half-light in the tower."

Marie Durand leaned in a half-sitting, half-lying position in the wagon; they had tried to provide some comfort with a few bundles of straw. She kept her eyes closed, exhausted and indifferent, as though her strength had carried her only to the conclusion of the ordeal and she could no longer cope with the end of it.

"Marie Durand," the commandant said, "here is the Prince de Beauvau. You know, the last time he did not come as your fellow prisoner, as you thought, but rather as your liberator."

She gave no answer. Now that all the torment she had suffered was over, evidently she was overcome by the wretchedness of her ruined life. With an almost indignant movement, she turned away. "She learned meanwhile that you are a Catholic", the commandant said by way of an excuse.

The Prince wanted to retort: No, I am not a Catholic at all, I am a freethinker—but he could no longer bring himself to utter that word—with irresistible force, he was overcome by the certainty that God is real.

"Marie Durand," he said, not concealing his distress, "yes, I am a Catholic Christian and as such one of those responsible for your fate—can you nevertheless give me your hand?"

She did not speak, obviously completely shattered. Suddenly the Prince saw her blind eyes open—her hand groped for her head. "God bless you, Prince", she said simply. Then the wagon started off.

When it had disappeared, the Prince turned to the young commandant and said to him slowly and gravely: "And now, my friend, take me as a prisoner into your tower."

The commandant looked at him uncomprehendingly, while the Prince calmly continued: "You are right to expect the royal mandate to release the prisoners, but I do not bring it. The King did not approve this release; it was based on my unauthorized order; it was illegal."

The young commandant paled. "Then," he said voicelessly, "then I am lost."

"I think", the Prince replied, "that you can save yourself if you take me prisoner. You will be acting quite properly if you do so, and I ask you to. Lock me up in the tower in place of the prisoners; do not hesitate", he continued; "I am sure of imprisonment in any case, and perhaps it is sensible right in this place."

The Chronicler can no longer vouch fully for what comes after that. In Aigues-Mortes itself, that is, in the little spot by that name, the legend persisted for a long time that they intended to keep Marie Durand back as the last of the prisoners, but the Prince of Beauvau volunteered to stand security for her, and he went to prison instead of her, and thus it does correspond to a deeper level of the affair. It is certain that he resided in the infamous Tower of Constance—we do not know how long—as he himself had wished. Was this Tower for him the mysterious prison that in reality was interior freedom, as Marie Durand had known it before him? Did he want to convince himself of this freedom, or was it his desire to make atonement that was decisive? We do not know; only the letter from the Marquise through which this imprisonment was brought to an end has been preserved. It contains the following lines:

> The King has consented to your unconditional pardon, Prince, and I do not think he will insist on re-arresting the prisoners—the pertinent order has been forwarded to the commandant. In order to save you, I had to remain for him what I have been to him for years: the mistress whom he repudiated in a moment of anger but soon intensely desired again to have at his side. In the night of love that I granted to him, everything was decided in your favor. Farewell, we will not see each other again. Reinette has delivered herself forever to the fate that separates us. For me there is no more pardon except for the awareness that you are saved by my final fall. My punishment is at the same time my absolution, the only one to which I still have a claim. For now I really have done for love of you what I once sought out of ambition—now I am, although forever separated from you, forever
>
> Your Reinette

In fact, the legal proceedings already initiated against the Prince were quashed, and there was no more talk about re-arresting the liberated prisoners. We know that Marie Durand and her companions were able to spend the last years of their lives in their modest homes. The Prince returned to his Governorship and dedicated himself to the duties of his office. In Paris and Versailles he was seen no more. For several years the rumor repeatedly surfaced that he had secretly become a Protestant because he remained unrelentingly concerned about improving the lot of the persecuted. The only one who perhaps could have corrected this assertion, Father Laroche, who is known to have visited the Prince several times, was expelled from France a little later with his Jesuit confreres and went abroad, where his trail disappears. Thus the Prince is surrounded on all sides by impenetrable silence—the rest of his life was spent as quietly and inconspicuously as the life of Marie Durand. He did publicly profess the Catholic faith, although some did not really believe this profession, and especially the philosophical circles of the freethinkers eagerly kept claiming him as one of their own. He did not think it worth the trouble to oppose those rumors. After his death, however, they found among his effects a prayer written in his own hand on sheets of paper that had been worn by frequent use; the lines on them read:

> My God, in Your inscrutable design you allowed those to whom You entrusted the faith of our fathers in our country to agree to persecute others who, in a time of atheistic blindness, professed the much-despised faith in You, although in a form different from ours. You gave them the strength to persevere in that faith while sacrificing their freedom, indeed often their lives; in an hour of

unscrupulous pursuit of luxury and success, You granted them the unselfishness to testify to Your praise in miserable prisons and on the galleys. You vouchsafed to them the everlasting renown of giving witness by their sufferings to the Passion of Christ. It pleased You, my God, to let them drain the cup of suffering to the dregs, so as to rouse from sleep my heart that was estranged from You —now may it please You also that this heart intercedes in turn for those who rescued it. Grant me the grace to profess this faith in You, Whom they gave back to this heart, in the Church of our fathers and, as a member thereof, to show love and respect for the persecuted, indeed, to declare until the end that we children of the old faith, too, are children of mercy. Help me to accept willingly the fact that my orthodoxy is doubted, so that I can make reparation for the crimes committed against the persecuted, which by human reckoning are irreparable. I repent of these crimes for my brothers and sisters to whom the grace of this repentance is still denied. And I commend the final reconciliation and union of all separated Christians to the assurance of Your infinite love.